OWNERSHIP

Written by

CAMO

DEDICATION

I want to thank my loving wonderful husband of 11 years for being there for me. If it wasn't for you, I would not have the time or strength to have accomplish my goals. Thank you, baby, for not giving up on me, I really need that foot in my ass.

To my three handsome sons and wonderful nephew who is like a son to me, thank you for your patients, understanding and love. This is what it takes to make your dreams come true.

To my immediate family, I love you all and thanks for your support.

To my friends...if you are my friend then you know who you are. No need to mention names, I could be wrong. But I will give a special shout out to my very best friend Tyonne who has been there for me and kept me focused. Thanks girlfriend we are friends for life.

Now, last but not least, I want to thank a very special friend, Author Keith Kareem Williams. You have been a godsend to me and a great mentor. Your patience, wisdom and shared knowledge has guided me to keep doing what I love to do. We are friends for life!

CONTENTS

Chapter One

Players Get Played

"Yo Kate! Hurry the fuck up with my face. It's taking you way too long for my make-up to get slayed. I know you do a bomb ass job…but yo! I got to go," Keisha shouts.

"I'm so sorry," I reply. "Today is a bad day for me and I'm trying my best to get it together. I'm almost done. All I have left to do is your lashes."

"Well hurry up, we got to go. Tonight, is a very special night and I want everything to be perfect. You did a slaying job on the other girls and I know you'll do the same with me."

"Shit girl! No doubt. I got you!" I say.

I did five frontal and make-up jobs today. Not only am I exhausted but me getting my shit together is weighing down on me. After losing my man two years ago for cheating with his enemy, my whole world came crashing down. Everyone lost respect for me. I lost, money, friends, family and most importantly…my man. Life was so bad for me I ended up smoking crack. Even though I am a crackhead, my skills for doing hair and makeup is like no other. I have a heavy customer base with clientele that makes my pockets heavy, but as soon as I make the money, I smoke it all.

"Ok Keisha, I am done with you," I softly whisper. "Now tell me what you think."

"Oh, shit bitch! Yo! You that bitch for real. All the niggas are going to solely be on my shit wishing they could fuck me."

"What the fuck you mean Keisha?" Deb barked. "We are all looking good, so all the niggas are going to be checking us ALL out. Not just you. Remember, there's no 'I' in team, so never just say

1

you."

"Shit, friend...why you taking this personally? I was just overstating how good I look, but you're right, we ALL look good," says Keisha.

"That's right, and I can't wait to get there tonight. We are going to have so much fun," says Deb.

"Yes indeed," Keisha agrees.

Keisha and her four friends Tasha, Candie, Deb and Vickie came to my spot to get slayed for tonight's event. Tonight's party is the night they have been waiting for. The Watson's Brothers host these huge events once a year at any given place or time. These two brothers, Jake and Johnny hang out with two other cousins named Stevie and Don. The four of them are the heads of the Watson's clique. They are some big balla drug dealers from Staten Island and they play the part. Women from all over wants to be with a member from this clique just so they can brag about who their man is and how much money they can get for shopping sprees. So, if any female is the lucky one that year, she better get all that she can 'cause next year, there will be a new chosen one. These men only keeps these girls around for one year.

Keisha, Deb, Candie, Tasha and Vickie add the finishing touches to their outfits. They are so amped about tonight they can't stop talking about it while admiring themselves in the mirror. All women are tall alike, same body structure and fine as hell. Being tall and slim has its advantages, especially when the whole clique is evenly the same. Compliments is a given. As they studied themselves vigilantly in the mirror and go over tonight's events the women are ready to go.

Pulling up in front of the club, my girls and I begin to go crazy. We are so excited by the throng of people and the way everyone looks.

"Oh shit!" Deb blurts out. "Tonight, is going to be on and

popping. I can't wait to get my sexy ass in there."

"No shit!" Keisha cheered. "Remember we are here for the prize, so let's keep our eyes on it."

"We got this!" I say.

When we exit the vehicle every head turns. Women and men stared so hard and it is obvious that we are the bitches of the night.

While attempting to approach the back of the line to stand, a tall, well-dressed, good-looking guy grabs Deb's hand and whispers softly, "You girls are too good-looking to be standing on the line. May I escort you ladies in?" Johnny smoothly asks?"

"I would be honored," Deb responds.

Still holding onto Deb's hands with a firm grip, Johnny passes through security, the throng of people inside and seats us in the VIP section. Johnny orders three bottles of Roederer Cristal Rose and tells Deb that he'll be right back.

Deb squeals with excitement after he walked away and says, "Bitches, I told you we look the shit. OMG! The niggas we came here for was not hard to find at all. We didn't have to look. They found us."

"Deb, everything is falling into place," Candie shouts over the loud music.

"I know girl, but let's not look thirsty even though we are. We must secure the deal. It's not over 'til it is over. So, let's get it."

While enjoying the scenery, dance a little and drank a bottle of Rose, three handsome, smooth men with Johnny in front approach the VIP. We women smile and extend our hands while Johnny introduces Jake, Stevie and Don to us.

"You ladies are drop dead gorgeous." Jake flattered. "Are you girls enjoying the party?"

Deb says, "Yes."

"I've never seen you girls before. Are you from the city?" Johnny asks.

"Yes, we live in New York. Each of us are from different boroughs, but we hang out with each other all the time," Deb answers.

"Well, that's just like us. We hang out all the time too. I guess you can say, we are each brothers' keeper," says Johnny.

"That's a good one," Deb laughs.

"The noise is a bit much down here and we would really like to get to know you ladies better. Would y'all like to come up to our private room? I promise I won't bite, but I can't say the same for them," says Johnny.

"I would love to! I won't bite either, but I can't speak for my girls," I reply.

Johnny and I laugh flirtatiously and follow the men to their private room. Walking through the crowd, all eyes are focused on us. Females are mean mugging 'cause they already know they are not the chosen one this year and niggas are staring hard, wishing they could taste all this honey. While escaping this heated space of people, we walk slowly through a long hallway 'til we reach the elevator. Johnny puts his key in the pad, turns the key and the door opens. We step inside first and the men follow with googly eyes, waiting to see what's going to happen next. Johnny pressed number two on the elevator pad and up we went. When the elevator door opens, there are two men standing there in black suits. Neither one of them smiles or speaks. They just stand there like mannequins.

As we walk past them, Johnny gives them a head nod and says, "No interruptions." They acknowledge his instructions and we proceed through the door. Once we're all inside, Johnny speaks and says "This is our spot ladies. You have to be very special to come up here, and by the looks of you girls, you are very fucking special. I can't lie, I haven't seen girls like y'all in a long ass time. So please make yourself at home and enjoy the night."

"So how many women have you invited up here?" Keisha asks.

"A few!" Johnny answers.

"So, let me ask you another question?" Keisha asks.

"Sure!"

"Why is it that women only last a year in your camp?" Keisha asks.

"Well, we try to give the ladies a chance to get some money," Johnny answers.

"What do you mean by that?" she asks.

"Well…let's just say, they do us favors and we look out," Johnny explains vaguely.

"Hmmm! So, all I have to do is ride your cock for a year and I'm set?" I ask.

"Basically, with a little extra," Johnny replies.

"Damn! You guys are something else. Just the thought of you

using women, treating them like hoes and throwing money in their faces paints a fucked-up picture of you," I tell him.

"How so?" Johnny asks.

"Well…let's revisit this topic at a later time, but I hope you are not expecting ass from us tonight. There's a whole party going on, music is pumping, and the crowd is doing its thing. This place is lit," Keisha interrupts.

"I agree, but our party is not down there. It's up here," he says.

"I hear that!" Keisha smiles.

The room fell quiet with hard stares amongst us. Jake offers us a drink to break the silence and summons the two bodyguards to come inside the spot.

As Becky watches the two men enter the room, she walks over to the bar wall and jokingly asks, "Where's the champagne Johnny?"

"We don't have champagne up here. We weren't expecting to bring females up here so quick. I guess you can say, we weren't prepared. Our bar is only stocked with hard liquor for shots and I'm sure you ladies want something fruity," Johnny answers.

"True!" I reply.

"Well, do you have any suggestions on what drinks you would like to have?" Johnny asks.

Becky walks up behind the two bodyguards and with a quick motion she reaches between her legs, detaches the Velcro strap, pulls out a small revolver and shoots the two bodyguards in the back of their heads, killing them instantly.

"Now Johnny…I suggest you to walk your fine ass over there slowly with your homies and pray you survive tonight," I told him calmly.

"WOW! WOW! WOW! What the fuck is this?" Jake shouts.

"Shut the fuck up! You know what the fuck this is. Now this is the shit that makes my pussy wet," I say.

"Yo! You won't be able to get away with what you're trying to do so let's just talk about this and we'll give y'all what you want and act like this never happened," Johnny pleads.

Becky busts two more shots in the ceiling while the rest of us aimed .25's to their heads.

Becky looks into Johnny's pleading eyes and says, "You know what I love about this room? It's soundproof. No one can hear you scream." Johnny eyes widen in shock as he wonders how the fuck she knew that. "So, sweetie," Becky continued, "I do believe we WILL get away with this. Now cut all this chit chat and open the fucking safe."

All the men stood there speechless trying to find the right words to calm the situation down, but every time they look at the dead bodyguards laying there, they are reminded shit is real and about to get realer.

"Okay! Okay! Okay!" Jake pleaded. "If I open the safe would you let us go?"

"Oh! I don't think so honey! You are going to meet your maker tonight. I can't believe how easy this was. Everything went faster and smoother than we planned it and you know why? Because, you niggas are thirsty for pussy. With all the money and clout, you still let pussy be your downfall. Shame on fucking you. All of you! Now open the fucking safe so we can go home."

Jake stands there with an equivocal look on his face, trying to wrap his thoughts around what is going on but can't make any sense of it. He tries to diffuse the situation by pleading to us to be easy but Candie shoots Jake in the head with no hesitation.

Johnny screams, "Don't do this please," and begs for us to stop, but as he keeps rambling on another head gets blown. Stevie falls to the floor and we laugh hysterically.

"It's only two of you left Johnny and you still haven't made any attempt to open the safe. You are a brother and a cousin short, so what are you going to do? I don't care for all this crying shit, as you can see. Me and my girls are about this shit! No fear, no pain and no love. So, get the fuck up and open the goddamn safe," I order him.

Johnny slowly gets up off his knees and walks over to the bar wall. He presses a button under the Ciroc bottle and the wall shifts to the other side. Johnny turns around and tries to plea with Keisha but before he could finish his sentence, another shot is fired, killing cousin Don.

"Too much talking," Keisha shouts. Johnny's shaky fingers begin to enter numbers on the keypad and the safe finally opens. "Good boy! Good boy!" Keisha says. Candie walks over and snatches Johnny by the collar, jabs her gun in his side and forces him to sit down. Keisha looks in the safe and finds three kilos of coke along with five hundred bands. "Not a bad lick," says Keisha.

Johnny looks up and says, "Now that you got what you want,

please spare my life. I will clean this whole shit up and nobody will ever know what took place here. To be honest this would be an embarrassment if anybody found out the truth."

Keisha says, "Fuck you," and lets off two shots in Johnny, one to his head and another in his chest.

Chapter Two

Cee-Cee

Head leaning back against the wall, standing straight up with a cigarette in my left hand, legs spread apart while my right hand grips the head. As my legs begin to tremble because my flesh is being sucked on, my lower body begins to gyrate on the face. This feels so good and my breathing is getting heavy.

"Ooooh! Yeah! Ahhh, keep it right there," I moan.

The cigarette in my left hand burns out, leaving nothing but ash because the vibe that I am on has my mind totally gone. I guide the head where I want it, hold it steady and let the tongue do its job. "Oh God, this shit is the bomb. Yeah…suck it, suck it. I'm about to cum. Lick all my cum," I whisper. As I feel myself about to explode, I let out a loud cry of, "Ahhh! Mmmh…drink it, every bit of it."

While hearing the last of the slurping sounds, I gently pull away. My knees are so weak, but I still hold my composure. I wipe myself off, reach into my stash and throw two dimes at Kate. She wipes her face, takes the dimes and runs out of my apartment.

Crazy crackhead bitch. One thing for sure, she can suck the spark out of a clit.

Kate is this crackhead that lives a couple of blocks from me. She is about 5'8," brown skin, very pretty with deep dimples, bedroom eyes and a banging ass body. Why she smokes crack is beyond me, but, hey, that's her thang. I'm sure if she ever left that shit alone, she would be a bad-ass bitch.

Ever since my man C-note got sent to the Feds to do five years, I've been letting Kate suck my pussy. I'd rather have a bitch doing that than some lame-ass nigga jumping on top of me. Besides, I can

8

bust a good nut for two dimes with no feelings attached. C-note doesn't mind at all because he knows his pussy is tight n' right, just the way he left it. He's only got a year and a half left and boy, I can't wait. I'm ready to be a wife and have some kids, but right now I have too much going on. Holding down the fort is a lot, but a girl got to do what a girl got to do.

After Kate left my apartment, I walk over to the closet and pull out my duffle bag. It contains five kilos of cocaine and two pounds of weed. I take a Cuban cigar from its box, slice it, and roll a fat-ass blunt. This weed is the bomb. It's homegrown from Antigua and it's nothing like the dirt they sell around here. I wouldn't dare give a nigga my ten dollars for a high I can never get. Besides, I get pounds of weed for free, and it's all for my personal use.

After taking a couple of tokes, I begin to feel real nice, so I put it down and chill for a minute. While I'm buzzing out on my couch, I realize it's time for business. I pick up my cell and auto dial this nigga name Tony from uptown.

Tony is the NIG-GA. When my man C-note put me on to him, he said, "Don't worry about nothing, Tony will do you right. Just give your shit to him and only him, and he'll make it happen." For the last three years, I've been giving him my work. He gets at least twenty kilos a week from me and his cut is two grand per kilo so he makes good money and I'm paid. I never ask him who his buyers are, and he doesn't know who my connect is or how it's delivered to me. The less he knows the better. This way, no one gets caught in anyone's shit. Tony is also quick. No matter what I put in his hands, within hours, I have all my money and not a dime less.

After Tony picks up the phone, he says, "Hey, Cee-Cee! What's the deal?"

"Nothing, hon. I got five on it."

"Aiight! I'm coming at you."

"See ya in an hour."

"One."

I hang up the phone, light my blunt again and get real mellow. My cell rings and as I look at the caller ID, I see that it's Stacy. Stacy is this chick that I roll with in Queens. She's black and Chinese, slim with a little ass and long straight black hair. Her pockets are fat but only because she sleeps with drug dealers. Stacy ain't like me. She's not an independent woman, but she's cool.

"What's the deal girl?" I answer my phone.

"Aw, nothing. Just wondering if you're coming out this way today?" Stacy asks.

"Yeah, I'm down for Queens. I need to get away from the city, but I gotta deal with something first. I'll call you when I'm done. Then, we can chill."

"Okay! Cool, but before I hang up, did you hear what happened last night?"

"Nah, girl. What?" I ask.

"There are these broads from the Bronx. I think, four or five of them, going around sticking up drug dealers and they killed the Watson brothers and took all their shit."

"Get the fuck out of here. Bitch what you say?"

"Word yo! These girls act like they're buying weight and when it's time to do the trade, they put guns in your face take your shit and end your life. It's serious out here."

"Well I don't have to worry about that because that ain't my line of work and C-note is in jail. Anyway, thanks for the tea and I'll holla at you later."

Oh! So, there's some wanna be stick up bitches, huh? Well it's all good 'cause I only fucks with one person and one person only. Stacy don't know what I do. She thinks I'm a booster and it's best she keeps thinking that way. C-note always says to keep people out of my business and don't be too flashy, and I try my best to do everything he says. Besides, I only have to be in the game until he comes home.

Time is running out, I jump in the shower, get dressed and wait for Tony. Tony is mad cool, fo-real. He's tall, about 6'2," brown skin, pretty eyes with a Caesar and deep-water waves. Tony is so fine that he sort of looks like a girl, but I know he is ALL man. All the girls around here love him, but he don't be giving none of them any play and it's crazy because he doesn't have a girl. He claims he's in love with someone and every time he talks about her, his eyes sparkles, but still, no one knows who this mystery woman is. He says he's saving all his money and when he reaches his goal, he's gonna claim his prize. I wish him luck. He has never mentioned her name and I try not to pry because it's personal, but I must admit, I am a little curious.

Buzz! Buzz! Buzz! My doorbell rings. I walk over to the door, look through the peephole and see that it's Tony. I open the door, greet him and he gives me the biggest hug ever. I hug back and let him in. He walks to the living room, sits on my sofa, reaches for the half of blunt that is in the ashtray and sparks it. I go to my bedroom, grab the duffle bag to show him what it's hitting for.

He says, "Cool! But Cee-Cee, I need to talk to you."

"What's up?" I ask.

"This is serious. I'm a holla at you when I get back."

"Well, if it's about those broads from the Bronx, I'm fully aware of the situation. This is not our concern because we are not a clique. No one knows about us. Right?"

"Hell nah! But that's not what I'm talking about. What I got to say is on some next shit. In fact, I wanna take you somewhere."

"Where?"

"What's your size?'

"What?"

"What's your size?"

"Tony, what's this?'

"Please, Cee-Cee. This is serious."

"Aiight. Eight."

"Shoes?"

"Seven and half."

"I'll be back in an hour."

"What's going on, Tony?"

"You'll see."

While I sit in my apartment and wait for Tony to return, anxiety begins to take control over me. I don't know what's going on and I hate being in suspense. I lay down in my bed, thinking of a hundred things at one time, when my phones rings so loud scaring the shit out of me bringing me back to reality. I answer and it's a pre-paid call from FCI Otisville. It's my man C-note.

I press five and the first thing I say is, "I love you daddy."

"Hey wifey. I love you too. Wha cha doing?"

"I'm just chilling waiting for my friend Terri to stop by," (we call Tony *Terri* because of the Feds phone. All the Fed's phone calls are tape recorded, so the female name is to keep it safe).

"Is Terri being a good girl?"

"No doubt! That's why we are how we are."

"I feel ya. So, are you coming to see me on Saturday?"

"I mean, do you really have to ask? I would come up there every day if I could."

"Baby, I miss you."

"I love you."

After we kicked it for fifteen minutes, we say our goodbyes and hang up. I pick up my cell to connect to my Bose Home Theater System, select H.E.R from my selection and decide to get prepared for what's coming up. I go to my dresser and apply MAC concealer, foundation, powder and blush to my face. I love make-up and the way I look with it on, it's like I am that bitch posing for the front cover of Vogue. Yeah…I look gud! I love my lips to be glossy because it reminds me of when I used to suck C-note's dick and how pretty they looked wrapped around it. Ummh…just thinking about it turns me on. I take off my boy shorts and wife beater, lotion up my body and spray it down with Givenchy, my favorite perfume. I put on Victoria's Secret nude sheer push-up bra and matching thong. I pin my hair up and release some Shirley Temple curls to give that sexy and slutty energy, that real *come fuck me* look. I put on my sheer Valentino robe and wait for Tony to come with clothes and money.

As I patiently wait for him to come back, I build another spliff. I love smoking weed. I love getting fucked up. I love for my eyes to be red and low. Point blank, it just makes me feel sexy. While sitting here getting fucked up and listening to the raunchy music of Chris Brown, I begin to feel sensitive; sensitive in a way to where I wanna be made love to. It's been three and half long years since I've been held by a man, and I'm longing for it. All I've been doing is letting Kate give me that pleasure but it's not enough. Hardly enough! I need to be bent up like a pretzel and dicked down hard. While I sit here getting depressed, I turned off the music and heard my doorbell ring.

I walk to the door and ask, "Who is it?"

"It's me." Tony shouted.

I unlock the deadbolt on the door and let him in. Tony stands in the doorway looking at me, and if I didn't know any better, his eyes were saying a lot. I turn and walk away, leaving him no choice but to get a full view of my voluptuous ass.

All I can hear is, "Umph! Umph! Umph. Is that all you ma?"

Now I am feeling embarrassed because I'm damn near naked in front of this man. I don't show it though and I answer, "All me, all C-note."

Tony twists his mouth into a smirk and passes me the money and the clothes. I go to my room, put the money away and try the clothes on. Tony bought me a Chanel body-con dress that fits like a glove. It stops mid-thigh and requires no bra. This shit is bad, worth all three grand and it's in my favorite color, pink. The shoes are pink, four-inch Chanel stilettos with a matching bag. After I gloss my lips with some more MAC lip glass, I was ready to go. I took one last look in the mirror, smile and blow a kiss to myself.

Coming out of the bedroom, I can't help but notice Tony's eyes on me again. They are saying something I don't wanna read, so I say, "I'm ready! Now where are we going?" Tony doesn't answer. He just leads the way.

Walking out of the building in silence, I can feel Tony's uncomfortable stares. Normally, I would feel flattered, but right now, I'm lovesick for C-note. I really want this night to hurry up and come to an end. Tony opens the passenger door of his 2019 BMW X7. The beige leather interior is as soft as butter. Yeah, Tony has a little style with him. This is the first time I have ever been in his car so I am quite impressed. Tony isn't dressed for the evening. He has on a white tee and blue denim Levi's and a pair of 95 Airmax. He's wearing an iced-up Rolex, a pair of diamond studs and a crazy ill diamond link with a heavy diamond cross on it that is set in platinum. It's nice and suits him well.

"So Tony, what do you need to talk to me about and where are we going?"

"We're taking a drive to Atlantic City."

"I don't want to gamble. Why are we going there?"

"We are not going to gamble. We are going to dinner and we'll talk then."

"How serious is this?"

"It depends!"

"Depends on what?"

"Depends on you."

"In what way and why me?"

"No more questions. Just smoke some weed, chill and relax to the music while we journey to AC."

Two hours later, we arrive at the Casino and walk in. We go out the back door to the boardwalk and walk down the strip until we reach the Ocean Casino Resort and go into the restaurant area. We sit at a candlelit table for two and order a bottle of Don Perignon. I'm happy about that 'cause this *longing for C-note* mood that I'm in has me in a need of a drink. Before we place our orders of lobster tails, shrimp scampi and snow crab legs, I already gulp down two full glasses and am ready for the third. As my head becomes wavy, the waiter comes to the table with our food orders and I ate like I haven't eaten in days. I guess this is the effect of drinking and I can't front, I really need to lay my head down. But, before we ride out, I need to know the reason why we came all the way up there.

"Tony, what is so important that we had to drive all the way out here to talk? What's up with you?" I ask.

"Relax baby! We'll get to me. Let's talk about you. No one knows anything about you besides the fact that you are C-note's girl," says Tony.

"Well that's all that anyone needs to know about me. My life is very simple."

"Cee-Cee, if I tell you something, can you promise me, you won't get mad at me?"

"I promise, now shoot."

"In fact, let's finish our dinner, drink some more and take a little walk."

"Aw man! You're beating around the bush. Just spit it out. You're starting to piss me off."

"I'm a tell you, believe that."

Tony ordered more Don and by this time I was lit. My head was fully gone, and I really need to lay down. I ask Tony to rent me a room and he said it was done. He pays the tab and we make our way to the glass elevator.

Standing in the elevator, I can feel my feet move from beneath me. I hold on tight to Tony and he holds me steady. When we came to the fifteenth floor, we walk five doors down and stop at the sixth. Tony takes the key card out of his pocket and lets me in. I clumsily walk my ass over to the couch, plop down in it and lean my head back. My head is spinning so much I don't even know if the room is nice or not. I just know that I am seeing double. I call out to Tony to get me a glass of water, and he does. When he comes back, he hands me the glass and sits right next to me. As Tony was about to say something, my cell goes off and I am too fucked up to get it.

Tony gets up, takes my phone out and says, "The caller ID says unavailable."

I say, "Oh damn, it's C-note. Can you please answer that for me?"

Tony responds, "Not tonight. Let the phone ring out."

By this time, I am so drunk I can't even argue.

"Cee-Cee, it's time to talk."

"Tony, I can't talk right now. I need some sleep. The DP got my head fucked up and I need to sleep this shit off."

"We'll, don't talk, just listen. For years now, I have been in love with you. I know C-note is your man and I know you love him, but I feel like I have no choice but to tell you how I feel. I think about you all day and night. All this money that I have saving is to take you out of the game and give you whatever your heart desires. I wanna spend the rest of my life with you, and if you give me the chance, you'll see how I can make a difference in your life. I know you just can't up and walk away from C-note, but in due time, you will be able to."

"Tony, you are bugging out bro. You got to be drunk. Just go to your room and sleep this shit off and we can revisit this in the morning."

"I am in my room," Tony whispers.

Before I can utter another word, Tony puts his lips on my lips. They are so smooth, so gentle and so warm. Am I so drunk that I'm thinking this is happening, or is it really happening? As I slightly open my eyes and see Tony's face close to mine, I try to shake him off me.

"No Tony, Don't! Please! Tony I can't."

I'm so drunk that my hands are too weak to fight. I try to push him away, but his full lips are all over mine, making it hard to speak or move him. Tony holds my chin and parts my lips with his tongue forcing his tongue to meet mine. As our tongues mingle and get to know each other, my guard immediately goes down and instantly I comply and return his kiss passionately. He strokes my face and pulls the pins out of my hair. When I pull away for a moment to catch my breath, he stares at me, touches my face and glides his thumb across my lips. I'm in a daze right now because I can't believe what's going on. Tony bends his head, kisses me and scoops me up off the couch. I throw my arms around his neck and rest my head on his collarbone while he carries me to the bedroom.

The bedroom is flawless. The lights are dim, the king-sized bed is round and beautiful and full of extra fluffy pillows. The air is room temperature and the mood is right. As he lays me down gently on the bed, I sit up on my elbows, drunk, watching him as he takes my shoes off. I lift my left leg and bend it so that my foot rests flat on the bed. My right leg stays stretched out.

Tony says, "Damn ma! You real sexy. Shake your hair out and let it land on your shoulder."

Lazily, I do what he says. Tony climbs up on the bed and slowly parts my legs a bit so that he can come face-to-face with me. He kisses my forehead, nose and sticks his tongue deep in my mouth.

"Ummp!" I moan as my elbows weaken, putting me flat on my back. Tony aggressively kisses me, and I suck the shit out of his tongue palming the back of his head. As we kiss for a minute our moans get louder and his tongue leaves from my mouth to my neck. "Mmmh! Mmmh! Damn this feels good.

Besides my clit, my neck is the next most sensitive spot on my body and he's fucking my head up right now. Calling out his name got him real excited. He moves his head lower to my breasts. First, he nibbles on the outside of my dress, getting my nipple fully erect. They are so hard and aching to be sucked. He holds them, molds them, squeezes them and teases them. Oh god! This is no good, but all good. My dress rises up exposing the inside of my thighs. He moves his hands down and in one motion, he got me up out of my dress. I am lying under him now with just a thong on. He rubs his hardness against my groin. He reaches for my breasts again. This time, he cups them and sucks them. He sucks them so good and hard that my nipples look like little torpedoes. I breathe with excitement. This shit feels so fucking good. I'm dying to reach my height. As he eases up off my nipples and kisses his way down my stomach, navel and inner thigh, he paints the outside of my pussy with his tongue. Slowly, he licks and flicks my clit with his tongue. After removing my thong to get a better taste, he commences sucking my pussy and giving me pleasurable head. My clit is so hard and my pussy is drenched with cream. I'm zoning. I open my legs wide and grind on his face as I palm the back of his head. His lips and tongue skillfully push back the hood of my clit and I lose control.

"Ummh! Ummh! Ummh! Wait Tony! Let it go! Tony! Please," I beg and moan. My legs shake and my body quivers and when he sticks his finger inside of me, I cum so hard screaming his name "Toooonnnnyyy!"

Tony locks his tongue on my clit and I aggressively try to push him away.

After he drinks every bit of my cream, he comes up, looks me dead in the eyes and says, "You belong to me. This is just the beginning."

Tony lays halfway on top of me and we both fall asleep.

Chapter Three

Cee-note

It's been three long years, and I have a year and some change left in jail. I'm overly anxious to get home to my beautiful future wife, my home, my business and time seems to be dragging. Not only is time dragging, but my woman is acting out. I'm hearing things about her that make me wanna kill a nigga. I keep wondering if I should believe what I'm hearing or if I should wait to hear what she has to say. Cee-Cee has never lied to me, but these rumors about her sleeping with Tony would make her a liar if it's true.

Tony...this fucking chump. Could he really get next to my woman? THAT, I can't see. This nigga is broke and lame. I know a nigga would be infatuated, but who would be? Cee-Cee is every man's dream. When you see her, your dick automatically rises to salute. She's 5'7, caramel-colored, nice, big brown eyes, shoulder-length hair, a tight round ass with a set of hips and breasts that are full and firm. She has half-dollar nipples, no stretch marks and a flat ass stomach. She will make you go home and tell your wife to get her shit together. Cee-Cee is bad. I've been with her since Junior High School. Her family and I are very close and they consider me their son-in-law. I promised that as soon as I get out, we are getting married and starting our family. We have more than enough money saved so we can invest and chill for the rest of our lives. This drug game gotta come to an end too. Even though we have been blessed with successful shipments, it's time to move on to bigger and better things. I've been doing some heavy brainstorming on how to become a billionaire, and by the time I get out, I will have mastered it.

In the meantime, my mind is not at ease. I can't believe that my woman has hooked up with the guy who is supposed to only get her product off. I will kill this nigga if he disrespects me and sleeps with Cee-Cee. Pushing up on my girl is a no-no. I love Cee-Cee and she will always be mine, til death do us part. I know she gets lonely sometimes, but that's why she has Kate. It's fucked up to say that it's alright for a woman to suck Cee-Cee's pussy, but I'd rather deal with that than a nigga pounding on my baby. Damn! Just the thought of a dude between my girl's legs, making her moan and groan, having her call out his name, makes the hairs on the back of my neck stand up. Shit! I'm ready to act the fool.

Cee-Cee got the sweetest, tightest pussy I've ever been in. I should know. I broke her virginity and I'm the only one that's been in it. Even though I've cheated on her a couple of time, it was nothing. Those girls could never win my heart, nor could they walk in Cee-Cee's shoes. I just did what I did because I am a man and I still came home every night. Cee-Cee is made for me. If she left me, my world would come crumbling down. None of this means anything without her. I don't know why I let her take on the business by herself. We have more than enough to chill, so I didn't really have to put her out there. Now, I could surely lose my woman over greed. Whatever is going on out there, I must give Cee-Cee the benefit of the doubt. I'm sure she's not going there. In fact, let me go call her.

Right now, I feel good after getting off the phone with Cee-Cee. I didn't bring up the rumors because I didn't want to seem insecure. She knows I got mad love and trust in her and we've come a long way. It would be crazy if I start questioning her now. I'm at the end of my bid and I know she can hold it down. As soon as I get home, I'm gonna drop this hot milk in her and produce my little girl. She wants that too, and it's time.

I'm trying to get one of these lame-ass officers to give me a room for a half an hour for three grand. I want to make my daughter now but, these chumps are so scared. Niggas don't have heart like they used to, but somebody will eventually want to earn this paper and when they do, Cee-Cee will be good and pregnant. God, just thinking about it makes my dick rock-hard. I want Cee-Cee and I need Cee-Cee now. As my dick throbs hard like a heartbeat, I close my door and put a towel around the outside knob. This lets the other inmates know that I'm busy. I reach for my photo album that contains only pictures of Cee-Cee. It got ass shots, negligee shots, bikini shots, masturbation shots and more. I open my locker, take out the Vaseline, get butt-ass naked, sit on my bunk and put grease on my dick. I open the album, and the first thing I see is a nice 9x12 face shot of her with full, glossy pink lips. "Umm...I love those lips." I put my dick in my hand and stroke it. I close my eyes and imagine her lips locked around it. I jerk and squeeze the head, play with it for some time and then stroke the whole dick. I look down at my penis and watch myself jerk my eight-inch cock from head to balls. I turn a couple of sleeves and see a nice ass shot. My hand starts moving faster and harder, and my moans get more intense. I must keep the loud sounds of pleasure to a minimum because I don't know who could be passing by my door. I call out her name softly, "Cee-Cee. Oh, Cee-Cee. Can you feel me mommy? You feel so good. I love your hot, tight, sticky pussy. Oh, Cee-Cee, ride this dick. Ride this dick that you so love." As my balls begins to tingle, I know I'm about to cum. I open my legs, lean back on the bed and fuck my hand. I fuck my hand in a frenzy while imagining that my baby is squat fucking me. Oh, God! This shit is feeling so good and I begin to explode hard. My body shakes and jumps as heavy loads of cum come out of my dick, leaving me exhausted. I lay there for a minute to catch my breath and then jump in the shower.

After getting myself together, I decide to call Pete. Pete is this nigga that's keeping an eye on Cee-Cee and recruiting all the females for our international runs. When I call, Pete answers and gives me some disappointing news.

"Hey Note. What's the deal?"

"You nigga! You're the one that's out there living it up."

"Well, you need to hurry up and get home or else you are going to lose Cee-Cee."

"Why you say that?"

"Because Tony got it bad for her. I was talking to some dudes the other day and they said Tony wants Cee-Cee and…something else, but I can't say over the phone."

"Is she sleeping with him?"

"Nah, but I hear it's supposed to go down tonight?"

"What? He's talking about fucking my woman tonight?"

"That's what I heard."

"Well, I can't believe that. If a nigga really wants to fuck Cee-Cee, he won't talk about it, so I'm a let it pass over my head. But you just keep your eyes and ears open. I want facts, not bullshit. Aiight nigga?"

"Aiight!"

"So, what the deal around the way?"

"Big shit happened. The Watson Brothers got robbed and murdered at one of their events last night."

"Damn that's fucked up, but that's their bad."

"I know that's right. Well I'm a call you sometime this week. So, one!"

"One!"

I hang up the phone mad as shit, 'cause I'm tired of hearing about Tony and Cee-Cee. I know my woman didn't fall and bump her head so, I'm going to sleep and I'll call her tonight before lock down.

After laying on my bunk restless as shit, I get up wash my face and make me a cup of soup. I feel a bit sluggish, but I need to walk around before the compound shuts down for the 10 p.m. count. I politic with some of the dudes and play a game of spades before I decide that it's time to call Cee-Cee. I walk back to the unit, and for the first time, the phones are clear. I jump on it and dial my wife. I call the house, I call the cell, I call the house and the cell again, but she's not picking up. I keep trying until the prison phones shut down. I go to bed damn near sick, worried and mad. All types of shit run through my mind and it gives me a big ass headache that needs more than Excedrin. I lay in my bed and pray that she's alright before I fall asleep.

Just waking up and it's morning. 6 a.m. to 12 noon was a repeat of last night. I dial and dial Cee-Cee's phone and don't get no answer. It's 12:15pm and this is the last time I'm going to call.

Ring! Ring! Ring!

Chapter Four

Tony

I just got off the phone with Cee-Cee, and I'm a meet up with her in an hour. She got some work for me and I got some plans for her. Tonight is the night to let her know exactly how I feel about her. We're going to Atlantic City for dinner and we're spending the night there. I haven't yet decided if I'm going to bed her, but something will go down.

Cee-Cee has been on my mind for the last three years. Ever since her man C-note introduced us to each other, I knew she was the one for me. It was hard to come at her in the beginning because that would have been a sucker move. Her man goes to jail and I take advantage of her vulnerability? Nah, that's not being a man. Besides, I wanted to make sure that when I stepped up to the plate, I could provide better than C-note because she's high-maintenance, in a ghetto way. Cee-Cee is a sexy, fly, businesswoman. What turns me on is how she holds her head high and is willing to ride or die for a nigga. I appreciate and respect everything she does pertaining to her business and her man. That's the type of woman I need by my side. I plan to take Cee-Cee out of the drug game. Once she tells me who her connect is, I can take over and step up the work. I will make her confide in me but first, I gotta get her away from C-note.

C-note is not a friend of mine. We just do business. When he knew he was about to do time, he asked me to help his girl out, so she could maintain. I didn't know who she was and when he did finally introduce us, I fell in love immediately. All I do is go out of my way to please her 'cause I'm trying to show her what kind of man I am. Cee-cee always asks me if I got a girl. I tell her no. I tell that I'm in love with someone, and we've always left it at that. She never pried even though I wanted her to because that would open a door for the beginning of *us*.

I'm nervous about tonight. Really, I hate rejection. Cee-Cee has never given me the impression that she likes me, but I'm a still try my hand. I'm not gonna take no for an answer. She's gonna be mine, and that's that. Romance is key, and I've got a whole lot of love to give. I'm so backed up, my balls are killing me. I have sex often, but it's always with these damn condoms. I can't bust a nut the way I want, and I refuse to take it off. No girl will get all of me but Cee-Cee. When I finally make love to Cee-Cee, that will feel like paradise and I'm gonna live there for the rest of my life.

I know me and C-note are going to have crazy beef. And…so what? I'm that MVP nigga and he don't have any wins. I don't have anything against him but I want his woman, his connect and the whole metropolitan area on lock. Soon, everyone is gonna have to come through me to possess and distribute. Ownership is what I'm hitting for.

Chapter Five

Reality

Ring! Ring! Ring!

Sleepily, I say, "Hello."

The operator says, "You have a pre-paid call from Otisville. If you wish to accept, press five."

I press five.

"Where the fuck have you been, and where the fuck are you now?" C-note screams through the phone.

"Baby, what are you talking about? I'm home."

"Girl don't play games with me. You are not at home, and why do you sound like you're just waking the fuck up?"

"What? Why are you buggin' out? Stop trippin'. I am at home."

"So, why didn't you answer the house phone last night? I called three times and I've been calling all morning. It's now twelve...no, it's after fucking twelve and you're just now picking up your cell phone."

"Oh baby! Last night, Terri came by and we went to Atlantic City, had dinner and I believe I drank so much that I passed out. I even had a crazy-ass nightmare on some sex shit with Terri. Can you believe that? I'm missing you so much that I dreamed the impossible. It's crazy."

"Well, I don't give a fuck what bitch sucks your pussy. I just don't want any nigga riding my kitten."

As I listen to my man talk that gangster shit I love, a strange feeling comes over me. Something is not right. While lying on my left side with the covers over my head, the sheets move. My heart races and C-note's voice becomes faint. I pull the covers down to my eyes and yell, "What the fuck? Where am I? Oh my God!" I drop the phone, turn around and realize that my nightmare is a reality and that I'm fucked. I pick up the phone again and start crying, "C-note! C-note! I'm so sorry! You are going to kill me."

As the phone clicks because his time has run out, all I hear is, "I told you baby, I'll protect you. You don't have nothing to worry about."

I jump out of the bed and tussle with the dress as I try to put it on. I don't wash my face or ass, but who gives a fuck. I got bigger problems than a crusty eye, stink breath and a sticky pussy. I got to go! As I haul ass out of there and jet to the lobby, I realize that I'm not the driver and that my bag and cell phone are back upstairs. Confused and dazed, all I can do is cry.

"Why is this happening to me? Why?" I walk up to a lady who was checking out and ask if I could make a quick call on her cell. After reading the concern on my face, she reaches into her bag and hands it to me. I dial Stacy to see if she could pick me up, but when I heard her voice, I decided against it. So, I just kept my conversation short. "Hey girl, what's up? I'm just calling to apologize for standing you up last night. Some people came by and invited me out to dinner, and that's how I ended up here. I gambled so much that I lost all my money, but I'm good. I'll call you tonight when I get home."

"All right girl make sure you do. Do you wanna hang out tonight?" Stacy asks.

"Nah, I gotta get some rest before I see C-note tomorrow?"

"Let him know he's well missed."

"Aiight, one!"

As I hang up the phone and slightly beat my head with it, I feel a shadow towering over me. I slowly turn around and see that it's Tony. He's well-rested, clean and smiling at me. Tony takes me by the arm and leads me to the elevator and then, finally back to the room. My heart is beating one hundred miles per hour and at this point, I feel weak, vulnerable and violated. Before last night, I was in complete control of myself, my business and my surroundings. Now, I'm all confused and hurt. How the fuck didn't I see this shit coming and how the fuck am I gonna explain this shit to C-note? I just gotta think.

Tony opens the door, guides me in and before I can say a word, he slams the door and startles me by making me choke on my words.

Tony walks straight up to me and says, "Don't ever disrespect me like that again. No woman leaves my bed unless I say so."

"Disrespect!? Nigga, you are the one who got me drunk and seduced me. That's disrespect! You are supposed to be that nigga to help me, not fuck me. C-note would kill you if he even thought you were trying to get at me. How could you? Tomorrow, I gotta go see him and he's going to tear that visiting room up when he hears about this shit."

"Cee-Cee, I don't give a fuck about C-note. I'm in the position to have you, own you and stop you from going up there to see that nigga. You are my woman now. Everybody will know and I'm not hiding it. You should be glad I didn't stick my dick in you because you would be pregnant right now. I got big plans for us, and no one is going to stop me. Not you and damn sure not C-note. I'm a let you visit that nigga and put money on his account, but that's all. You and I are a team now. Not only are we going to be hood rich, we're going to be filthy rich. The female I always talked about and said how much I love...is you. So, don't play yourself and don't hide from me. Don't make a situation be what it shouldn't be. Now, go wash your funky ass."

Tony reaches down to kiss me, but I turn my face. He grabs me and forces his tongue down my throat and says, "All of this is mine, whether it stinks or not."

After a good cry, a shower and some lunch, I am ready to go. I gather my things and wait for Tony to open the door when my cell rings. I look at the name and say, "Damn, I hope it's not C-note. I'm not in the mood to explain shit right now. He will have to wait 'til tomorrow." As the name reads unavailable, I say, "Fuck it!" Let me answer, "Hello."

"Wha ah gwan? Me ah call yah cell all night an yuh nah answer yah cell. Da dam phone ah ring, ring bloodclatt ring."

"Oh shit! Buddy! I forgot to call you last night. I got so much shit on my mind, and right now is a bad time for real. I can't talk."

"Well, tell me something. Do yu wan me feh come dey, ah yu ah gah come yah?"

"I'm coming down there. I need a break, so I'll call you tonight with all the details."

"Cool scene."

I hang up the cell and put it in my bag and walk out to the car.

While driving in silence, my mind drifts on Buddy.

Buddy is our connect from Antigua. Nobody knows about him but the four of us...me, Brother, C-note and Pete. It's best this way because shit is dangerous out there and it' better for me 'cause I don't wanna do time. Dealing with Buddy is the bomb. Anything I want, I get just as long as I get the people to get the goods out of the country. We only pay $5000 per kilo. Who the fuck can beat that? We have a nigga named Pete who recruits the people and everything is sweet. No busts and no problems. Buddy got the best shit too. Pure Columbian Cocaine. When I get my shit, it's wrapped airtight in a block and it has the official Columbian seal stamped on it. When a nigga be talking about, he got a real brick, he really don't. He just got 36 ounces in powder form.

Brother! Oh brother is really my brother. He too, is doing time. He's at Allenwood Low and will be coming home at the same time as C-note. He and C-note caught this case together. They were hit with five years for gun possession. The Feds couldn't get them on drugs, so they hit them up on guns. Brother and C-note are the perfect team. They are so laid back and about money. Long money! When they were home, they were moving two hundred keys a month. It was sick because we only paid five gees and sold them for twenty-five. We more than tripled our money. When they got locked up and told me to carry on the business, I said I couldn't handle all that weight by myself, and I didn't trust anyone. C-note said he had a man uptown that could handle twenty keys a week and that I should deal with him and only him. That man was Tony. He suggested that I rent a bullshit apartment uptown and be simple. No one knows about my real life or where I live but the five of us...Brother, C-note, Buddy, Pete and me.

As I snap back to the situation at hand, I realize that we are in front of my building. I open the door and get out without saying a word. I just want to run upstairs, scrub his scent and touch off of my body. Even though he didn't sex me, just the thought of his tongue on my clit makes me sick. As I walk to my door, I realize that this nigga is on my heels. I turn around and say, "I need time to myself. Call me later and we'll talk some more."

"Don't play games with me, Cee-Cee. This is the real deal."

I run upstairs, lock my door and cry myself to sleep.

It's 7 pm, and I'm just waking up, feeling hungry as shit. I walk over to the fridge and see everything I would love to cook, but I'm not in the mood to do so, so I pick up my cell and dial the Chinese restaurant down the block. I order shrimp fried rice with lobster sauce, and a side order of crab Rangoon with extra duck sauce. I give them my address and they give me a delivery time of twenty minutes. After hanging up, I decide to check my voicemail and handle my business.

While listening to my voicemail, I deleted the unimportant ones and saved the ones that needed to be saved. I go to my closet pull out the money machine and grab the duffle bag that is supposed to contain $115,000. Tony takes his cut up front so, what he brings back to me is all mine. I put the money in the machine and as usual, all the money is there. I go shower up again and put on my favorite True religion jeans and the matching T-shirt that bares my midriff. It is perfect for showing off my belly ring and waist chain. I put on my pink Louis Vuitton clogs with the brown LV logo all over them and my matching oversize satchel. I pull my hair back into a ponytail and apply make-up on my face. I must admit, being ghetto fabulous is fly, but I really miss the real me.

My doorbell rings and it's the deliver guy. I take my food, pay him and give a large tip. Those niggas love coming to me. If my order is eight dollars, I hand them a twenty and let them keep the change. Next, I put some music on and of course, I blast "Ready to Die" by the Notorious B.I.G and ate. Now that I am done eating, I walk over to my stash and build a big blunt. I jam to Biggie and buzz the fuck out. When I realize time is beating me, I grab my nap sack, lock everything up and bounce. Tonight, will be a long night, but I am ready.

Leaving my building to hail a cab, in no time one pulled up in front of me. I get in and tell the driver, I'm headed to Long Island. The Hamptons. He asks for some money up front. I asked how much, and he replies, "Ninety dollars." I give him $120 and we are on our way. After a few moments of silence, the driver tries to make small talk. He's funny and entertaining, but I let him know from the door that I have a man, so don't go there.

As we approach my exit, I direct him. I hate giving people my address up front because some driver's memories are photographic and in my line of business, I can't chance it. All he hears me say is, "Go straight, turn left, and make a right," things of that nature. Then finally, we stop. I get out and watch the driver drive away until I can no longer see his cab.

While walking my sexy ass in this high price neighborhood, I begin to feel relaxed and powerful. I walk about five minutes and stop at Yepton Mansion. I love this house. It has fifteen bedrooms, twenty bathrooms, a movie/media room, a music studio, a physical fitness room, a library, indoor and outdoor swimming pools, a sauna, three Jacuzzis, four fireplaces, a six-car garage, a tennis court, indoor and outdoor basketball courts and more. Yepton Mansion is crazy. Everyone who is anyone admires it, and it belongs to me. My world! My life! Real life.

I run up the walkway, punch in my security letters (BBCC), and my front door opens. I step in and close the door. Instantly the door locks. I exhale and say, "Home sweet home." I run up my spiral staircase to my master suite and I am greeted by Pus-Pus, my all white Persian cat with huge green eyes. She jumps into my arms and I carry her to my walk-in closet. Inside my closet is my shoe wall, and under a pair of Red bottoms, is a numeric keypad. I punch in the eighteen security numbers, which is mine, C-note and Brother's birth dates. The whole shoe wall moves, and the vault door opens. This vault is as big as a standard size master bedroom and reeks of the fresh scent of money. There is over $500 million in cash and $50 million in jewelry in here. I take the money out of my bag and stack it up according to denomination. I open my jewelry box and take out a pair of thirteen karat diamond stud earrings, my fifteen-karat diamond choker, a thirteen-karat princess cut tennis bracelet and my twenty-karat diamond platinum engagement ring for tomorrow's visit. I close the case and walk out. After I press end on the pad, the shoe wall automatically closes. I go to the phone, check my messages and dial American Airlines. After making reservations for my trip to Antigua, I call Buddy with all the details. As usual, we don't talk much over the phone, so the convo is kept short.

After hanging up with Buddy, I decide to get my clothes ready for tomorrow's visit with C-note. My jewelry is already in place, so now I gotta get my gear right. I walk back over to my California closet, scan through my clothes and pull out my baby blue Donna Karen two-piece suit. The coordinating top is haltered and extra tight. It has a plunging V-neck that exposes my cleavage. Then I take out my Jimmy Choo stilettoes and sunglasses. I wash my hair, roller set it and sit under the dryer. I realize that I am exhausted. It's now eleven o'clock and I really need to clock some zzz's. I walk over to my oversized bed, take my clothes off and lay in my nice, neatly made bed. Oh yeah! My bed has been calling me for weeks. I turn my head and see a clip in the ashtray, so I spark it. Smoke fills the air instantly and Pus-Pus purrs, letting me know she is buzzing too. I smoke and relax, feeling real mellow and sexy. I put out the clip, turn off the lights and try to go to sleep.

While tossing and turning, trying to find the right spot on my bed, my cell phone goes off. *Who the fuck could this be and why the fuck are they calling me now?* I get out of bed, run to where my bag is and answer the call.

"Hey Tasty," the caller said.

"What?"

"Hey Tasty."

"Who is this?"

"The same nigga who sucked that sweet, tasty pussy last night."

"Tony."

"Yeah Tony. Where are you? I'm in front of your building ringing down your doorbell, but you're not here."

"Well, I'm at my friend's house in Queens."

"Are you coming home? Or should I come pick you up?"

"Nah, I'm spending the night here because my friend is riding with me to see C-note tomorrow."

"Well, where she at? Let me say hi to her."

"No, I'm not going to put her on. What? Are you trying to keep tabs on me?"

"Nah, I just wanna make sure you ain't with no nigga. That's all."

"Well, we need to talk. I think you're getting beside yourself. What happened last night was wrong. Dead-ass wrong, and I'm mad as hell. We can't do that anymore."

Before I can say another word, I hear click. *Did this muthafucka just hang up on me?* I wonder. Oh well, I'll just go to sleep. But as I tried to doze off again my cell rings.

"Hello."

"I'm back now. I couldn't talk before, but I am ready now."

"Tony."

"Yeah, listen Cee-Cee. I don't know what part of my English you didn't understand, but I'm feeling you. Not only am I feeling you, I'm in love with you. From the first time C-note introduced me to you, my heart, mind, body and soul said you are the one for me. I ache for you every night and now I can't hold back any longer. You're mine and it's a done deal. So, you just got to make up your mind and surrender because I...AIN'T...LETTING...YOU...GO! Now tell me something."

"What?"

"What are you doing?"

"I'm in my bed, laying down, trying to get some sleep."

"Hold on!"

I hear him put the phone down and heard some rustling in the back. In less than a minute, he says, "I'm back. I just took off my clothes and now I'm lying in the bed too. Where is your friend?"

"She left with her man."

"Oh yeah!"

"Yeah!"

"Cee-Cee close your eyes for a minute. In fact, keep them closed while we talk."

"My eyes are closed. I'm tired, and I'm ready to say goodnight."

"Why you got to be so damn difficult, Tasty?"

"Stop calling me Tasty."

"Aiight! Just vibe with me. I want you to imagine that I'm right there with you. I'm down by your feet sucking on your toes."

"Tony, I'm not going to do this. We are not going to have phone sex."

"Shhh... just close your eyes and let me talk to you. Free your mind of all thoughts and feel my mouth sucking on your toes one by one. How does that feel, Tasty?"

In a low voice, I say, "Nice."

"Tasty, part your legs a little bit and let me kiss your toes and lick all the way up to your inner thighs. Let your imagination run wild with mine. Let me feel your love."

As I can feel these kisses, my legs open. They even open wider than a little bit.

"Tasty, now I want you to take your right hand and play with your nipples. Slowly and softly palm the whole breast and squeeze pinch your nipples. Get them hard for me."

"Ummmh! Ummmh! Come suck them Tony."

"Yeah Tasty, work with me. Are you feeling me?"

"Yes Tony."

"Now Tasty, move your hand lower to my sweet pussy and rub on it."

"Ooooh! Ummh."

"Tell me what it feels like, Tasty."

"It's sooo… hot and wet."

"Good! Just rub the outside baby and don't go in. Tasty, right now, I got my hard-ass dick in my hand and I'm stroking it too."

"How big is it Tony?"

"Ten inches and thick as a python."

"Ooooh, that sounds so good."

As I rub my pussy, it gets wetter and wetter.

"Tasty, I wanna eat your pussy. Open up baby and let me suck on your fat clit. Put your finger on it and rub it like I'm giving you head. Can you feel my mouth on it?"

"Yes Tony. Ahhh...Ooooh…Ummmh."

As Tony listens to my moans, his moans increase. He tells me how he's stroking it. Long strokes from head to balls and short four-inch strokes on the head.

"Oh God Tasty! You got me feeling so good. All this dick is yours. I can't wait to give it to you. Oh God! Your pussy is so tight, warm and sticky. I love sucking your pussy. I want my dick to go in now. Stick two fingers inside and work it slow."

"Ah! Ah! Oooh baby."

"Yeah Tasty, I can feel it. You got a tight fat, creamy pussy. Can you feel this dick?"

"Yeeessss."

"Well fuck it. Ooooh…yeah…Tasty! Like that. Yeah, yeah, yeah. I'm about to cum."

"Me too."

"Fuck harder," I cry and we're both panting, moaning and fuck-talking our way to pleasurable, intense orgasms.

Tony says, "In a matter of time, your mind, body and soul will belong to me. We're gonna say goodnight, but as soon as you get back tomorrow, call me."

"Yes, Tony."

I roll over and go to sleep with Tony on my mind.

Chapter Six

Intrigue

While sitting in the visiting room waiting for C-note to come out, all eyes are on me. I'm the definition of perfection. Niggas, bitches, CO's, mothers and fathers all want a piece of me.

As my fine ass man enters the visiting area, I meet him halfway with a big hug and long kiss. Immediately, I feel his dick rising, so I slow motion grind against it. As we pull away because the CO's are hating, I can see we are the center of attention. We sit down, and before I can say another word, C-note takes my hand in his and squeezes the shit out of it, making my body cringe and my eyes water.

"Cee-Cee, are you fucking Tony?" C-note asked between gritted teeth.

"Oh my God! Baby, why would you think that?"

"Because that's what I heard and that's the fucking rumor out there. I called Pete last night and he said that Tony took you to AC and that y'all spent the night up there together in the same room. It kind of make sense to me because I called both phones and you never answered. Plus, Pete said Tony is going around saying he's out to take my woman. What the fuck is up with that?"

"Baby, I'm not fucking Tony. Yes, I did go to AC and I told you that. We had separate rooms right next door to each other, and then I came home. I don't know where Pete is getting his information from, but you can't go around believing muthafuckas. I love you, and only you, and I would never do anything to hurt you. You only got a year and a half left. I've been letting Kate pleasure me, so why would I stop now?"

"I don't know! But I don't want any problems, and neither should

34

you. Tony is only there to work for you, not fuck you. That's it, that's all. Cee-Cee, I will kill a muthafucka for you. Don't put me in a position to come back to jail. Hold your head up and represent me to the fullest. Don't give a nigga the satisfaction to say he fucked my wife, ya heard."

"Yes baby. I know."

After everything simmers down, we eat, drink, laugh and get down to business.

"Cee-Cee, did you call Buddy?"

"No, he called me. I told him I'm going down there. I made reservations to leave Wednesday and return the following Wednesday. Tomorrow, I'm going up to see Brother. He said he needs to discuss some things with me before I leave. I'm not sure what it is, but I'll find out tomorrow."

"Are the girls ready?"

"Yeah, they're leaving the day I get back. Everything is sweet."

"Does Tony know about our business?"

"Hell no! Stop overthinking. I'm much smarter than that."

"I know you are. Just keep a level head."

"Oh yeah! Before I forget. They got some stick-up bitches from the Bronx that's targeting all the top-notch drug dealers. They are coming off with crazy weight and if you ain't giving up the drugs and the loot, then you are one dead muthafucka. I heard these bitches are bad, fine and nothing nice to fuck with."

"Well, we won't have that problem."

"I know! Thank God for that, but I won't hesitate to bust my guns."

"Yeah, ok. Now give me a kiss."

It's three o'clock and it's time for me to go. We stand up, hug and suck each other's tongues. C-note's dick rises again and it feels so good on my navel that I wish I could kneel down and shove it in my mouth. Damn! Wishful thinking. As we stand there grinding on each other, the CO signals for us to be easy.

"Hurry up daddy, I need you home."

"I'm trying. Just don't give my pussy away."

"It's all yours."

After we kiss our final kiss, I pull away, walk out of the facility and into the parking lot. I get into my gray, 2019 fully loaded Escalade that's sitting on thirty-twos. I crank my system up and blast my music all the way back to the city.

While driving to the city, feeling good and looking fly, my mind begins to drift. I start thinking about my encounter with Tony and the rumors that are already flying around. I can't believe Pete would tell C-note some shit like that. Why didn't he pull me to the side before taking it to C-note? You just wait 'til I see his black ass. As for Tony, I can't wait to check him on telling niggas that he's gonna take me away from C-note. What the fuck is on his mind? I'm fucked. This can't be happening to me. How am I going to handle this situation? For a nigga who ain't knock my box, he got some shit with him. Thank God Tony and I never fucked, but I must admit, the foreplay we had was off the hook and I want more. I can feel him. I wanna go there, but I can't. C-note will go crazy. I mean the world to him, so what am I going to do? As I begin to think more about it, my body receives a tingly sensation and it's for Tony, not C-note.

The last two days have been intriguing. Tony got my mind open. One night, he sucks my pussy so good that I adopt the nickname Tasty. The following night, he brings me to an orgasm by having phone sex. I want him. I know this is against my man's wishes, but I gotta bed him one time. A one-nighter can't do any harm, right? As I entertain the thought more, my pussy gets moist, and my clit gets hard. It's so hard that it feels uncomfortable. My mind is telling me to call Tony, but I can't have Tony see me like this.

While driving back through the hood, I pass by my area. My windows are rolled up and darkly tinted. As I lean back and drive, who do I see? Kate. Yeah, I'm get my pussy sucked now. Right now! I roll down my window a little and shout in a husky voice, trying to disguise myself.

"Kate! Yo Kate!" I shout.

She comes up to the window and peeps through. Her eyes light up when she sees me looking like the millionaire I am.

"Get in, but don't open the door too wide," I say.

"No doubt ma," she says and hops her ass in real fast. "What's the special occasion Ma, 'cause you are looking real good and rich? Do you have a hot date?"

"Nah, I was just cruising and then I saw you."

My clit kept getting harder and harder, letting me know I needed her to kiss it.

"Yo Kate, we're going to park this truck, run up to my apartment and have a little fun, okay?"

"Anything for you. I love sucking your pussy. I think about it all the time."

"Nah, you don't think about my pussy. You think about the crack. You really need to get off that shit and fix yourself up. I'll help you anytime you're ready."

As I park the truck, I tell her to get out and run upstairs. I waited five minutes then proceed to my building at top speed. I don't want anyone to see me looking the way I do. When I get up the stairs, we enter my apartment and she sits on the couch. I go in my room and bring out some weed for me and some crack for her. I hand her two dimes and roll me a blunt. While she sparks up her pipe, I light my blunt and get nice and sexy. I slowly come out of my clothes and sit here in my thong and ice. I watch her continue to get high and then when she felt her buzz, she comes over to me, pulls my thong off, spreads my legs apart and kisses my clit.

"Ummh" I moan

I tell her to take her time and eat my sweet pussy. She opens my legs wider, giving herself complete access and full view of my pussy. In goes her tongue, nice and slow with a long deep lick.

"Ooooh!" I moan.

Kate takes the tip of her tongue and licks every part of my sweetness…inside the lips, around my hole and inside my hole. She scoops my clit into her mouth and my body jumps. The sensitivity on the head is beyond anything I can explain, and it drives me wild. "Ooooh, Kate! That feels so good. I love the way you suck my pussy. Ahhh…Ahhh…Yeah!" As I begin to gyrate on her face, her tongue is steady sucking on my clit. "Damn girl! You give the bomb head. You'll get a bonus tonight."

Kate spread my legs wider, licks my pussy, scoops my clit, licks my pussy, scoops my clit and then suck, suck, suck my clit. While I moan, grind and grip the back of her head, all I can hear is slurping sounds. She is sucking me so good, too good that's is hard for me to catch my breath. Her head bobs up and down between my legs and I wanna scream, but the pleasure won't let me. I hold her tight and grip the couch, her hair, her shoulders, my hair and my breasts. I mean, just about anything I can think of touching, my hands are reaching for. As my clit gets harder and swells, my body shakes uncontrollably. "Oh God Kate, I'm coming," I scream and moan loudly as my pussy's hot cream runs all down her throat, chin and neck. Kate knows to suck all my cream and when she was done, I fold up in a fetal position on my couch without moving for about ten minutes as I wait for my clit to contract back to its normal size. When I finally collect myself, I go to the bathroom, wash up, put my clothes back on, light my blunt again and relax. Kate also got herself together and instead of giving her more crack, I give her two hundred dollars. I can see in her eyes that she wants to smoke, but I would rather give her the money.

As I walk Kate to the door, she turns around and says, "I need to holla at you."

I shut the door and say, "What's up?"

"Cee-Cee, the word is out that you are Tony's girl."

"I'm not Tony's girl and I wish everyone would stop saying that."

"Well, whatever is going on, be careful. Tony is not a nice person. He will break you down to size. Tony only cares about himself and he will do whatever it takes to get what he wants. Don't let the good looks and the charm fool you. One more thing, don't tell him anything about me."

"I hear you and what you say to me stays with us only. He won't know anything about you and thank for the heads up. If anything was to ever happen to me, you tell Brother and C-note what you know and they will take care of you well."

"Thanks for the money Cee-Cee and I'm gonna take your advice and clean myself up. That's my promise to you."

"Alright girl, I'll see you around."

I close my door and decide to relax in my apartment. I don't feel like driving back up to the Hamptons. I'll smoke some more weed and chill indoors for the night. It's a four-and a half-hour drive to see Brother, so I need some rest. I pick up my cell and call Stacy.

"Yo bitch! What's the deal?"

"Nothing! Chilling-chilling. I'm just here sipping lemonade while sitting in the shade, smoking purple haze."

"I hear that, hot shit."

"Gurrl...Dem chicks from the Bronx done struck again last night. They came out to Queens and hit them cats up in Queens Bridge."

"Word. What did they get?"

"They came off with fifty keys, one and half mill, all their ice and girl you wouldn't believe...they tied them up, pulled their dicks out of their pants, taped their dicks to their hands and shot them dead."

"Oh shit! They left them with their dicks in their hands. Yo, that's some crazy and funny shit. Those bitches are serious. So, who are they?"

"Girl, no one knows."

"You see, that's what those cats get. Every pretty face they see they be trying to fuck and look what happen. You would think that now a nigga would keep his dick in his pants. You get it!" we laugh.

While we vibe some more on the phone, my cell beeps.

"Stacy, hold on. My cell is beeping, someone is trying to call." I answer and it's Tony.

"Hey Tasty, what's up?"

"Nothing."

"I thought I told you to call me when you got back."

"Yeah, I know, but I had something to do."

"Okay, I'll be at your place in a minute."

I click back over the phone and tell Stacy that I got to go and hang up real fast. I run into my bedroom, hurriedly take my clothes and jewelry off, put on some shorts and a wife beater, and wait for him to knock. He knocks, and I unlock the door to let him in. Tony grabs me and kisses me with such passion that, this time I did not resist. When he pulls away, I close the door and we sit on the sofa.

Tony looks around my apartment and says, "It's time for you to buy a condo."

"I don't want no condo. I wanna stay right here."

"Why? This place is a dump. You got money out the ass, and you wanna live like this."

"I don't have money like that."

"What? You sell keys. In fact, what do you do with all your money?"

"It's not my money. I get paid just like everyone else, and I have a lot of bills to pay. My family is fucked up and I gotta help them too. So, it's not what you think. Besides, I don't want to discuss my financial situation with you."

"So, let me buy the condo for you?"

"No! C-note is not having that."

"Fuck! Fuck! Fuck that cornball-ass nigga. He doesn't have you on lock no more. I do! If his ass was so much in love with you, he would have bought you a house, a car, iced your ass up, and stacked your fucking bank account lovely. But nah, his love got you living fucked up. What kind of man is he, leaving his so-called wife fucked up? Huh! You shouldn't have to hustle. But hey, I'm a let you tell me when you're ready to play the part. Until then, I'll lean back. Soon enough, you will forget all about C-note. Once I stick this dick in your ass, it's a wrap."

"Yeah aiight. This is the problem; you always go to take shit to the extreme. You act like C-note did you something. You are the one who is fucking with his prize. So, be easy! Anyway, I gotta go to bed early tonight. I'm going to see Brother tomorrow."

"How are you getting there?"

"Stacy's man lent me his Escalade, so I'm a drive myself up there. When I took her home, he said I can chill with his ride until Monday."

"Why is Stacy's man lending you his truck? What's up with that?"

"Ain't nothing up with that. What's wrong with you tonight?"

"You would love me if you would just let me take care of you the way I want to. You better make up your mind soon about being my Queen B. I'll have you iced up being the baddest bitch uptown and driving a sick whip. I want my woman looking right representing me. All you gotta do is say yes, and after tomorrow, I don't want you driving the next man's shit. Aiight!"

"Aiight! Anyway Tony, I heard these Bronx girls are wildin' out. They really got those guys good in Queens Bridge last night."

"Yeah, that's their bad."

"All I'm saying is to be careful."

"I don't have to be careful. Only one woman can entice me, and that's you. Now, give me a kiss."

After an hour of talking to Tony, we decide to say goodnight. I walk him to the door, and we kiss like lovers, rubbing our bodies close together. I think, by now, he knows he can hit it. Whatever he's up to, he is definitely taking his time. Yeah, I'm open. Real open.

"Tony, before you leave, can I ask you a question?"

"Yeah Tasty."

"Why haven't you made love to me yet?"

"Yet!" Tony smiled. "You want me to?"

"No! I'm just curious. I mean…you went down on me, and we had phone sex, but you never attempted to make love to me."

"Tasty, to be honest…you're not ready for me yet. You ain't ready for what I have to give and you ain't ready to give me ownership. Our foreplay was just an introduction to my love, but when I decide to let the anaconda loose, a lot of things will change, and you won't have no choice but to submit. Believe me, I want you in the worst way, but I can wait. Control is key and soon the time will be right. Just be ready 'cause there's no turning back."

We kiss again. He leaves and I go to bed.

Chapter Seven

Being Naughty

Today is the day I go to see Brother. I can't go up there looking all slutty n' shit, so I'll try my best to look like a schoolgirl with a little sex appeal. I styled my hair in two Indian braids. I don't wear any makeup, but my lips are glossy as hell. I put on a light pink and grey Gucci sweat suit with a pair of Gucci sneakers. I'll wear my ice from yesterday but change my bag and shades to Gucci. After kissing myself in the mirror, I am set to go.

I get in my ride and crank up the bass with some Beyonce, Alicia Keys, and of course, Keisha Coles. The block is quiet 'cause it's 4:30 in the morning but who gives a fuck? New York never sleeps. I thump my sounds all the way to the George Washington Bridge. After I pay the toll and pass the GWB, I spark my blunt and cruise all the way to the prison.

As I pull up at Allenwood Low at 8:15 am, I see there are a lot of people there already. I walk to the lobby, sign in, wait for my number to be called and of course to get searched. This is the most frustrating part. I don't see why we must go through this bullshit because fo-real, fo-real, nobody is that crazy to help their peoples plan an escape.

THE FEDS DON'T FUCK AROUND! If you try that shit, then this is your permanent residence, so ain't nobody that stupid. But then again, you just never know what crazy-ass muthafucka may decide to try the impossible. A nigga who's doing life might chance it, but if he gets caught, then he and his people are ASSED THE FUCK OUT.

After passing the bullshit security, I sit and wait for Brother to come out. As usual, he's always the last one so I go to the vending machine and buy up all the hot wings (these are his favorites), and I chill some more. Finally, this nigga comes strolling his tall ass in with a huge grin on his face. I guess he can sense this cussing I'm about to give him.

"Brother, why the fuck you gotta always be the last one to come down?"

"Aw sis give me a hug. You know your brother gotta make a grand entrance. I'm so muthafucking fly. I love for all the socials to be on my shit."

"You're so conceited."

"Not conceited sis. Convinced!"

As we laugh and hug, I had to admit that my brother is fly. His swag is definitely on point, even in his khakis. Brother is 6'5, very slim, brown skin and sort of looks like Tupac, but don't tell him that or he'll flip…but he's very handsome. All the girls love Brother and he loves them too.

"So, bro…what's the deal? Next year, you'll be coming home, so what you got in store?"

"Sis, we'll get to my business in a minute. First, what the fuck is going on with you and Tony? Are you fucking the worker, AKA the hired help? Aw, hell no! I know my sister is bigger than that, right? That nigga is lame. Real lame. Look at what you're sitting on. If you're gonna fuck around on C-note, then do it right. Get a nigga that has more paper than him. Not just any chump. I'm surprised sis. This ain't you at all. You ain't thinking with the upstairs, you're thinking with the downstairs. Tony is only good for business. That's C-note's people, so you can't play him like that. Besides, I don't like that nigga. Something about his ass ain't right. Be careful sis."

"Brother, I am not fucking Tony. Pete shouldn't have told C-note that shit. By the way, who told you that?"

"Pete."

"You see that nigga is spreading lies on me. Maybe, he wants to fuck me and is jealous my friendship with Tony. That's all that it is."

"Well, I hope so. You know C-note is like a brother to me. So his beef is my beef. Niggas don't want none, and you know this. So, don't put someone's family through a grieving process because your ass is hot."

"Anyway, I came up here to talk about business, not gossip."

"Funny! When are you leaving?"

"I'm leaving Wednesday and coming back the following week. I got the girls set up already and everybody knows what they got to do."

"Okay! Well, I want you to push more weight. How many girls are going down?"

"Five."

"Good! We got a new compressor, and this one will compress a key to the size of an 8x8 notebook. I want each girl to bring back six. Buddy already knows what to do. Okay?"

"I'm with that."

"Pete is recruiting more and more girls. I want you to step up his pay. Give him two g's per girl. He's real good and he's got a way with them girls."

"Yeah, whatever."

"Yeah, whatever what? Pete is getting paid to watch you separately and he's got bigger shipments to get through that you can't handle that comes in from the port. So be easy on him. He is our eyes and ears and we don't want you to be taken advantage of."

"Yeah!"

When the visit comes to an end, we hug and say goodbye.

On my way back to New York, I decide not to go uptown. I need to put the truck up, store my ice and pack for my trip. A one-week vacation requires a lot…fourteen outfits, fourteen pairs of shoes, seven bikinis, numerous pieces of lingerie and my jewelry box. The only thing I don't have to bring is money. I have three bank accounts down there and of course, I deal with the plastics. Once the packing is done, I am ready to go. Tomorrow, I'll get my hair done in some twists at Mo Hair Salon. It's just too damn hot down there for curls. I'm trying to be as comfortable as possible. This is not all pleasure…it's mostly work with a little play.

As I pull into my driveway, I realize that I am really tired. Driving back and forth to PA always stresses me out. I open my door, crawl upstairs and lay on my bed. Pus-Pus comes running up to me and snuggles in my arms. I'll just take a nap and eat dinner later. While resting for what seems like only a minute, I fall into a deep sleep that knocks me out until ten the next morning. I get up, turn on the Jacuzzi, and soak my body for forty-five minutes. I get out, get dressed and make some breakfast.

While eating my French toast, eggs with melted cheese, grits and bacon, I gulp down two full glasses of orange juice. Damn! This feel good. I chill around the house making sure everything is packed up. I'll be leaving from here, not from uptown. So, I'll be back Tuesday night for my Wednesday morning departure. Now that I have everything situated, it's time for me to call an Uber. The car arrives and I'm on my way to Mo Hair Salon. I know this is gonna take all day. Two strand twists can take at least eight hours and I don't want two bitches on my head. For three hundred dollars, each twist better looks the same.

It's now twelve midnight and I'm just walking out of the salon. I must admit, I look the fucking bomb. Those island niggas are going to go crazy. I check my messages on my cell because I had it on silent. When I am doing something, I like to do it without interruptions. Besides, I was reading this bomb ass book called "Death in the City," by Keith Kareem Williams, my favorite Author. As I listen to my messages, I can't believe that all of them are from Tony. Tony is straight cursing me out for not answering my cell. Since he wants to be so nasty, I'll make him wait some more. He ain't my man, so I don't have to respond. He better not get on my fucking nerves. Shit! I may not call him 'til tomorrow.

I hail a cab, make a stop at Micky D's and from there, head to the building. As the cab pulls up in front of my building, I am shocked to see Tony's BMW parked and him sitting in it. I tip the driver, walk up to his car and tap the window. The look Tony gives me is enough to kill me. He gets out of the car and follows me up the stairs in silence. I can feel the heat of his eyes on my back, and it makes me feel uncomfortable. We walk to my door and enter my apartment. Tony goes straight to my couch, sits and mean mugs me.

"Tony, what's up? Why are you staring at me like that?"

"Where have you been?" he asks, ignoring my questions.

"I went to get my hair done. Do you like?"

"Why didn't you answer your cell all day?"

"I kept the cell on silent and I just checked my voicemail. I was going to call you when I got in."

"Why didn't you come home last night?"

"After I gave Stacy's man back his truck, we chilled, and I spent the night over there."

"Call Stacy."

"What? I'm not going to call Stacy. What the fuck is wrong with you? I don't like people keeping tabs on me. If this how it going to go down, then maybe we should be easy. I don't want anybody trying to run my life. Besides, we are trying to get to know each other. Do you already doubt me?"

Nah, I'm just saying, you're always talking about this girl Stacy and I have never seen this person."

"Alright, to kill your suspicion, we'll go to Queens tomorrow and I'll introduce you to her."

"Well for now, come here. Stand in front of me and pull you pants down and show me your panties."

"What?"

"Let me see the crotch of your panties."

"Why?"

"Just do it and open your legs."

I don't know what the fuck is going on, but I just do as he says. Tony examines the crotch of my panties. Then, he runs his right hand up my leg and sticks his index finger deep in my pussy. It hurts a bit because it's been a long time since I've had a man's finger inside of me while it's dry. Tony takes his finger out and smells it, he looks at me and says, "Okay, pull your pants up."

"Why did you do that?" I ask.

"I wanted to make sure you didn't fuck on me. That's all. Now, I know your scent very well, so don't ever try no slick shit."

"Tony, I haven't been sexing anyone. It's been three and a half years and if it wasn't for you coming on to me, I wouldn't be thinking about it now."

As Tony watches every move I make around the apartment, I begin to feel horny. To break his silence and stare, I ask him if he wants something to eat. He says, "No, but roll me a blunt." I roll the blunt, sit next to him on the couch, and eat my Micky D's. As soon as I finish eating my food, I take the blunt from him and smoke, smoke, smoke. I really don't do that puff, puff pass shit. I just smoke until I feel nice.

"Tony, you wanna watch TV or listen to some music?"

"Listen to some music," he answers.

I set my Pandora to the Kelly Rowland station and "Motivation" came on.

"Aw shit!" I say and we both smile.

"Tony, I'm going to take a shower to wash the loose hair off my back. I'll be back in a minute."

"Aiight!" Tony says and continues smoking.

I walk out the room, and watch as Tony leans back and vibes to the music. The music sounds so sweet and relaxing from a distance. I go to my room and strip down. I walk to the shower, turn on the water and let the steam fog up the room. I step in and the hot water feels so good as it beats on my body. Sitting in that chair for eight hours really took a toll on me, and I need this. I take my loofah, lather up with Givenchy body wash and slowly wash my body. While scrubbing my body with my face up towards the shower head, I feel a cool brisk of air on my back. I turn around and see that it's Tony. He gets in with the blunt in his hand. The music is still blasting, and every song, so far, is a fuck me song. I turn all the way around to face Tony. My nipples are fully erect, and my body is half sudsy. As my eyes peep out his whole body, my mind says, "this muthafucka is mind-blowing and his dick is every bit of ten inches." His chest is cut the fuck up for a slim dude. He has a six pack and a pelvic V, and the definition of his body is shaped like a cobra. His dick hangs thick and heavy and the head really does resemble a fish head. FAT AS FUCK. Tony takes the loofah out of my hand and passes me the blunt. While standing here smoking, Tony washes my body. He washes every part of me gently. I'm so fucking turned on that it don't make no sense. I gotta have it. As he washes between my legs, my clit throbs, and my pussy creams the fuck up. I go to touch him, but he takes the blunt out of my hand and says, "Rinse off."

"My eyes widen like, "Wha?"

He says it again, "Rinse off, and when you're finished, you can go dry off."

I hurry up and rinse off mad as shit. I get out and he hands me the blunt then shuts the shower door in my face. I am so heated, frustrated and turned on that I could cry. This nigga got my pussy on fire and won't put the flames out. I sit at the edge of the bed and smoke until I got real fucked up and when I was about to get up to lotion, spray and slip on my negligee, he comes out. He has a towel wrapped around his waist, and he looks so damn good. He walks up to me plants his lips on my lips. Without hesitation, I tongue him aggressively. He pulls the back of my tight twist and shoves his tongue down my throat and rub his hardness across my groin. "Mmmh," I moan. In my head, I'm screaming, "Fuck me," and if I didn't know any better, I could have sworn he heard me. He removes his tongue from my mouth, and I gently kiss his chest. His chest is so tight and cut. I take the tip of my tongue and trace every cut that lines his six pack. When I get to his pelvic V, I slowly remove his towel and let it drop to the floor. I look up at him, hoping he won't stop me. I grab his dick, hold it in my hand, massage it, caress it and stroke it. As his dick grows in my hand he says, "Kiss it." I get down on my knees, jerk his dick some more, then kiss it. I kiss all over the head and shaft. I lick from his balls all the way up to the tip of his head. I lick the rim of it and then put the head of his dick in my hot, watery mouth. "Ooooh," he moans and touches my face, caressing it as I suck the head of his dick. As my tongue licks and sucks his head, I grip his shaft firmly and jerk it up and down.

"Ah Tasty," he moans. Tony leans back his head and starts slow motion grinding in my mouth. I'm steady sucking his dick. My mind is telling me to control it, take over, and freak the shit out of him. Since I can't get him to fuck my sweet pussy, he's gonna fuck my deep throat. For each time he grinds, I let his dick slide further and further into my throat until my bottom lip touches his balls. "Oh, my God! Tasty...How the fuck...Ahhh...Ooooh...Ahhh," he cries. As my throat stretches to accommodate the size of his python, I throat suck his dick. I come up and down, fast and slow, from head to balls with a tight mouth grip. I cuff my lips over my teeth and go to work on him. Tony cries out my name, "Cee-Cee! Tasty! Oh God Baby,

Suck it. SUCK IT MOM-MY…I-ANI'T-NEVER-HAD-ANYONE-SUCK-MY-DICK-LIKE-THIS-BEFORE…OH GOD! OH GOD! OH GOD! THIS FEELS SOOOO FUCKING GOOOOOOD."

As he pants, grunts and damn near cries, I give him what he wouldn't give me. His legs tremble, and his ass tightens up. Without easing up, I bob my head up and down, round and round, and finger his balls. He grips the back of my head and fucks my mouth harder. The way he is putting his back into it, you would think he is fucking some pussy. "Mmmmmh, mmmmh, mmmmmh," is all I can moan, and his moans, screams and cries get louder. Tony applies more pressure to my throat, then grips my shoulders and lets out a loud cry before gushes of thick cum floats down my throat. I bob my head faster and suck harder and he continues to cum feverishly, screaming standing on his tip toes looking all sick and deranged. I drain and drink every drop of his cum. I suck until his dick went limp. I get up off my knees, leaving Tony standing there, fucked-up and sweaty. I go to the bathroom, brush my teeth and lay in my bed. When Tony finally, comes off of his high and is able to speak, he sits next to me and compliments me on the best head job he has ever received. He talks about it for fifteen minutes and I know that I have fucked his head up. Tony rolls another blunt, and we smoke lying in each other arms.

"Tony."

"Yeah Tasty."

"I forgot to tell you that I have to go to Virginia for a week. My grandmother is real sick and we're taking turns watching her. I'm leaving Wednesday and I'll be back next week."

"Do you want me to come with you?"

"No! You can't come with me. They will definitely have something to say about us. Are you forgetting that I'm C-note's fiancée?"

"Cee-Cee, let me ask you a question? Do you honestly think I'm going to keep letting you see C-note? Do you honestly think I'm going to be the one to take the loss? Nah Cee-Cee, not me. You got one week to get your mind right. When you come back, we're going to finalize our relationship because I'm taking things to another level. I want complete ownership."

"Tony, we need to slow down. We are playing a dangerous game. Can't we just have fun until it's time for C-note to come home?"

"Cee-Cee, you haven't heard a word I said, have you? I'm not down with OPP, I'm for ownership. I love you, and you ain't going anywhere.

"But..."

"But nothing...I don't want to talk about this anymore. When you come back, you will know what everything it's hitting for. Anyway, are you leaving work for me or what?"

"No, I put everything on hold until I get back."

"That's a no-no, Cee-Cee. Nothing gets put on hold. You just wait 'til you get back."

As we smoke some more weed, cuddle and kiss, I begin to feel horny.

"Tony, make love to me."

"No, you ain't ready for that yet. You'll be ready when you get back."

"I'm ready now."

"Cee-Cee, when I enter you, you will be all mine. Ownership...remember? That's not a word to fuck with. Are you ready to be my woman?"

"Why you got to go there?"

"You have one week to get your mind right. Now go to sleep."

Chapter Eight

Vacation Nightmare

I can't believe I almost missed my flight. Fucking around with Tony could have cost me a lot and put me in some serious shit. Buddy would have flipped if I didn't make my trip. To him, being on point is a must. Buddy is very superstitious. Well, that's what I call it. He calls it being safe. He would have said, "This is a sign of bad luck," and would have put everything off for another time. That means I would have had to reschedule all the girls' flights and it would have been chaotic. One thing for sure, I got to be easy with Tony because I'm slipping and I need to get a grip. I can't let this little escapade with him fuck with my state of mind and interfere with business.

Relaxing on the flight is something that is very hard for me to do. I love to travel but I'm scared to fly (I hate heights). So, I mediate and pray that this three-and-a-half-hour flight will be safe. I lean back in my seat and rest my eyes. I am tired as shit and I doze off thinking about Tony. What am I going to do? Why am I falling for him? This is gonna cause major problems in my life. I gotta stop it and stop it now before it gets out of control.

C-note's beef is my brother's beef and that means double trouble. I got one week to get my mind right and keep this on a professional level, take it back to where it was before that night in Atlantic City. It's not like I came on to him or made any promises. I can't control his feelings for me. They were there before I had any knowledge of them. Now, all this foreplay is blowing my mind and we haven't even had sex yet. I guess I should be glad for that because being head sprung on some dick is not a good thing. I got a man that's coming home in a minute, so I can wait. It's not that serious but, who am I fooling? I'm enticed. I want it and it's not fair for me to go through this. I know I'm gonna cheat and what's so fucked up is, the nigga I wanna cheat with wants to create a problem. He can easily ride this hot, wet, pussy for the next eighteen months, but nah…he wants to claim this ownership shit. Man fuck it! I'm just gonna leave his possessive ass alone. Business is business and we ain't mixing business with pleasure.

While I sit here having this self-talk, time flew by and it is time to land. I gather my things from the overheard compartment and make my way to the exit door. I love being in first class. Not for the complimentary treatment, but to be one of the first ones to exit the plane. When the flight crew member opens the door, I am met by the sweltering, salty heat. Instantly, perspiration drenches my clothes. I walk down the stairs and walk this long-ass strip outside in the blazing sun to get to the terminal. I hand my passport and declaration form to immigration and they stamped it with a two week stay in the country. I walk to the baggage claim area and wait for my suitcases to arrive on the belt. As the luggage belt begins to move all the Red Cap boys come in and surround the tourists.

Red Caps are the men who help the tourists with their luggage and they get tipped very well. While the men watch the belt go around, they all spot my signature-made suitcase. It is white with gray initials BCB all over and they all reach to grab it. I walk over to them and ask, "What is going on and why do we have to go through this every time I come here?"

"One of the guys by the name of Keith says, "Cee-Cee, yah dun no it's me turn to carry yah bag."

"So, what's the problem?"

"Me nah hav no problems. Ah dem wid the problems. Dem always wan all deh money and dey no yu ah gah give big tip."

"Well, all I want is for Keith to handle my luggage this time and if this is going to be a continuous problem, then I'm gonna assign one person to work with me. Seen!"

Keith pulls the rest of my luggage from the belt, puts them through customs and once everything clears, we walk outside. Once outside of the terminal, I hear my name being called. Keith points in the direction of the voice calling my name and its Buddy. I wave and he quickly walks towards me.

Buddy is something else. For a man who is fifty-five years of age, this nigga got his shit together. If you didn't grow up with him, you would think he was thirty-five. He's in good shape and fly as hell. He is the ice man and one sharp muthafucka. All the ladies love him, but he won't commit himself to one woman. However many women he has, believe me, they all know about each other and are content with it.

When Buddy gets to me, he hugs me and tells Keith to put my stuff in his truck. When Keith comes back, he hands Buddy his keys and gets a fat-ass tip. I'm sure that was the biggest tip ever. I told Buddy I want Keith on the payroll to receive me every time I come through and that I want him to be my personal driver. Buddy says, "Okay!" and tells Keith to come up to the house tomorrow. Keith nods with excitement 'cause he knows he's about to get paid.

While Buddy and I walk up to his car, I compliment him on his custom-made 2019 Mercedes AMG CT Coupe. This shit is bad. It's metallic blue with cream leather interior, fully-loaded and the steering wheel is on the left side so, I know I'm driving that. I just say, "Pass those keys, youngin' and let the big girl roll."

"Jus tek it easy an nah crash mi shit," he says.

"Would I do a thing like that?" I ask, smiling.

We cruise all the way to his mansion in Parham. This place is so huge. I could live here with ease. It has ten bedrooms, five bathrooms, two bonus rooms, two pools, three Jacuzzis, a tennis court, basketball court, a bungalow for visitors, eight car garage and everything else you can think of. This is just one of his mansions in the Caribbean islands. I love it. When I told him, I wanted to stay at the St. James Resort, he was not having it. Besides, C-note told him to keep me close.

When we enter the mansion, it feels so good and the temperature is moderate. Not too cool with the air-conditioning and not too hot from the heat; just right. He asks me if I'm hungry and of course, I reply, "Yes." He shouts to his cook Erma, tells her to make me a plate of food and bring some Vitamalt and Ting to drink. Buddy already knows my favorite island drinks. When Erma brings my tray of food, it is full of everything I love…curry shrimp, seasoned rice, fried dumplings, boiled plantains and a plate of salad. "God! This is good." After eating the whole tray of food, I still had room for more but instead I settle for a bowl of coconut rum ice cream and that put the finishing touch in my belly. I sprawl out, put my feet up and light a cigarette. While smoking and chilling out, Buddy takes the cigarette out of my hand and says, "Smoke dis instead. Yah dun no me nuh like deh cigarette smell. It tink. But dah weed me luv, so uno can light up all day and night and me nah mind."

So, I smoke on the good ganja weed and pass the fuck out.

I must have slept for hours 'cause Buddy just woke me up and it's 11 pm. I take a shower and put on my two-piece gray Nike spandex outfit that shows every single curve of my body. My stomach is exposed to show off my belly ring. I have on my gray and white Nike sneakers and I'm just right for the night. I go downstairs and find Buddy in the living room. He says, "We are taking a drive." I go get my bag and we are on our way.

Antigua is beautiful. The night is quiet and the stars are so bright. Even when the reggae music is blasting hard, the place is still so peaceful and very different from the states. It's like paradise. Passing through the towns and waving at everybody makes me feel like a celebrity. In fact, that's how I feel. When you are in the company of Buddy, you feel like that because he is well-known and so am I. Everyone loves me. As soon as they see me, I get a warm welcome and I love it.

As we drive further to the country, we come to a stop and pull into a long driveway, right up to the garage door. We walk in, pass through three doors and enter a room that has three men in it. The three men are named Pint, Young Mon, and Juni. These three men are already grinding blocks of kilos in the grinding machine. We put masks over our noses and mouths so we don't catch a contact high. I walk over to the new compressor and see that it is designed to flatten, shape and package the coke anyway you want it. In my case, I need it to be a quarter of an inch thick with a little flexibility and 8x8" wide. Since my girls carry these drugs on their bodies, it must be done right. It must be made to look like it's a part of their bodies.

"Cee-Cee," Buddy shouts. "How much stuff yah need and how many girls ah come?"

"Five girls are coming a day apart from each other and Brother wants them to carry six a piece. Two on the legs, two on their stomachs and two on their backs."

Buddy tells Pint, who is tall and slim, to get undressed. Then, he tells Juni to take six packages and tape them on Pint accordingly.

When Pint was all taped up like one of the girls, Buddy says, "Get dress and move around like if yah nah hav nutin'."

Pint does as instructed and not only am I'm impressed, I am amazed by how this new compressor makes a big difference. Fo-real, fo-real, if I wanted to add more, I could, but I'm not going to be greedy. If anything, I would step up on the girls, but as for right now, this is enough.

Buddy calls my name again and asks me for the female's photos. I reach in my bag and hand them to him. He scans them and passes them over to Young Mon. Young Mon takes them and puts them in his pocket. He's the one that is responsible for picking the girls up from the airport, showing them around the Island, getting them back on their flight and making sure they stay on the flight. He does this so that if one of the girls decides to double back, he can deal with the situation at hand. It would be a sad situation if one of them ever tried to rob us. When the plane is up in the air, he phones Pete to let him know that Antigua end has made it through.

After a couple of hours pass by, I realize that I am tired as shit, but I can't complain because I'd rather handle my business from the door than procrastinate and since everything is much easier and faster, I can spend the rest of my days having fun, fun, fun. So, if I have to stay up all night, then so be it. The guys are compressing two hundred kilos and Buddy doesn't want to leave until everything is done. I can't blame him because, even though his men are loyal, Buddy don't put anything past anyone.

Buddy is not afraid of stick-up men. He has so much clout that if anyone tried to rob him, they might as well kill him. The word would get around and niggas would be so pressed to work for him that they would drop a dime. The reward for your head would be so heavy you would give up your own mama, especially if it's US currency.

Now, the police...Buddy loves them all. Of course, he would. They are on his payroll, the whole force.

While the last batch of keys is being compressed, we clean up everything. Buddy hates sloppiness. I clean the machine, sweep, dust, and I mop. We take the two hundred keys, put them in a dungeon under the garage and lock up.

It's four o'clock in the morning, and we are heading back to the mansion. Sticky, powdery and tired, I stroll my ass to the shower and smoke some weed. I figure I'll have an early breakfast and sleep until late in the afternoon.

As I got up later that day, I feel so good and well rested. I'm energized and ready to hang out. After getting myself together, I put on my white Prada bikini with a mini wrap-around skirt. I slip into my Prada slides, some platinum and diamond jewelry to compliment my outfit. I take my twist and put it in a ponytail and leave my face plain. No need for make-up in this heat, but the lips have to stay glossy. I grab my oversized Ralph Lauren beach towel and head to the sitting area where Buddy is.

"Buddy, are you going with me to the beach, or shall I drive myself?"

"Yeh, me ah come. Peppa Pot ah play down by Fort Beach, so we ah gah go dey."

"Cool, cause that means my friend Tutu should be there too."

Tutu is a friend of mine who goes with one of the members of a Calypso Band named "Peppa Pot." She has a daughter with this guy and she feels she is the cream of the crop. Everywhere he goes, she is on the set, thinking she can stop anything from happening, meaning, (keeping the girls away) but he is so fucked up. He don't give a fuck about her. Plenty of times he has talked to females right in front of her. One time, Brother and I went to one of the Peppa Pot shows because truthfully, their shows be the bomb. They are the number one calypso band in Antigua. After the show, Tutu decides she was leaving with her man by the name of Biggah. She walks up to the car and noticed a female in the passenger seat. When she told the girl to get out, Biggah jumps out of the driver's seat and said, "Me ah fuck dis gal tonight." Brother and I just looked at each other in shock and could not believe what we'd heard but what was even harder to believe was that Tutu got in the back seat of his car. I don't know why she did that but, Biggah gave her the ass whooping of her life. I have never seen no female get kicked all up in their chest, neck and face. It was fucked up and would you believe she still didn't get out of the car? She just cried, went home with him and made love to him like nothing ever happened. The next day, when I saw her, she could barely talk, and her face was black and blue. I didn't say anything about it, but I knew a nigga could not have done that dumb shit to me. Brother would have killed him. This happened years ago and they are still together today. I can bet any amount of money she'll be at the jump off.

We pull up at the beach and it's crazy crowded. All different types of people are here. Rich, poor, black, white, Chinese and tourists out the ass. Everybody loves Peppa Pot. We park and pass everyone trying to find a spot, so we can chill.

"Cee-Cee, yu wan some ting feh eat?"

"Yeah, get me some fried fish, bread and a couple bottles of Ting."

I find a spot and lay my blanket down and listen to the sweet music of calypso. As Buddy returns with the food, my cell rings. I answer and it's Tony.

"Tasty, it's Tony. I miss you baby. When are you coming back?"

"I've only been gone for a day. You know my grandmother is sick and I need to stay a little while."

"Well, I'm sick too and I can't go to the hospital."

"What's wrong with you, Tony? Whatever it is, it can wait until I get back."

"No, I need you to come home now. It's a matter of life and death."

"What?"

While Tony and I are talking, Buddy shouts, "Cee-Cee, hurry up an eat dah food before it gets cold."

Tony screams, "Who the fuck is that? I knew your ass was with some nigga. You trying to play me bitch? I got something for that ass."

Before I can respond to his accusations, my phone goes dead. Fuck! This is the last thing I need, but there is nothing I can do about it now, so I set the phone down and continue to have a good time and eat my delicious food.

In the wee hours of the morning, we're still at the beach. When the Islanders have a beach party, it's a never-ending affair. As long as people are there, the music don't stop, but I'm getting tired. With the hot weather, body heat and crazy weed smoking, I am over the top and I need to lay it the fuck down. As we're leaving who do I finally see…Tutu. She's drunk as shit and looks a mess.

"What ah gwan?" Tutu asks.

"Nothing. I'm just chilling, vibing to the music and now I'm about to go lay down."

"When yah come?"

"I came yesterday and I'm leaving in one week."

"So, when me an yu ah gah hang out?"

"Soon."

"Alright, hurry an call me."

"Okay, I'll check you later."

I make my way to the truck, get in and doze off until we get to the house. I go to my room and put my cell on the charger, pick up the phone and dial Stacy. I know Stacy is going to wild out but fuck it. I'm a call her anyway. I ring her cell and she picks up on the fourth ring.

Sleepily she answers, "This better be important."

"Hey girlfriend! Wake the fuck up."

"Cee-Cee."

"Yeah."

"Do you know what time it is?"

"Yep, and I don't give a fuck. I just walked in the door and the first person I thought of was you."

"Well, how nice. How is your grandmother? She can't be all that sick if your black ass is just now walking in the door. You should have taken me with you. We really would have a had a ball."

"Grandma is sick, but I can have some fun too. Once I put her to bed, then it's all about me."

"I hear that."

"Bitch…major shit went down. It's hectic in the area."

"Word!"

"Gurrl, the Bronx stick up chicks are doing the damn thing. They are all over the news. We still don't know who they are. All we know is that it's five females."

"What? What is going on?"

"Well, from what I've heard and seen on the news, those bitches ran up in Larry's spot down by Coney Island. They murdered him and his four workers. One of the guys let off a shot and got one of the girls before he died."

"What?"

"Yeah girl. They don't know where she got shot, but they found a different trace of blood. Those girls came off crazy big this time. The Coney Island spot is the main base, so they did the damn thing."

"Oh my God! Larry is dead. This is bad news. Real bad news. I know his family very well and I can just imagine how they feel. I'm sure the funeral will be in a couple of days, so I gotta come back."

"What are you gonna do about your grandmother?"

"I'm a ask someone in the neighborhood if they can watch her until one of my family members gets here."

"Do you want me to come with you to the funeral?"

"Yes, that would be nice. I'll call you in a day or two, okay?"

"Yeah…One."

I hang up the phone and cry hysterically. I bawl so loud, so hard and so much that I hyperventilate. I can't believe Larry is dead. He is Brother right-hand man, so I know Brother is fucked-up right now. Oh Brother, just hold your head. I'll be there soon. I pick up the phone and dial American Airlines and change my return flight to Saturday. I make another call to Keba, who is Larry's wife. I don't talk long, just enough to give her my condolence and to let her know I will be at the wake. I quickly call Stacy back and let her know when I will be home. In the midst of my confusion, I smoke some weed and go to Buddy to explain why I have to leave much sooner than I planned to. Buddy understands and assures me everything is set and ready for the girls to come. I go back to my room and lay down.

A few minutes later, Buddy taps on my door and says, "Pick up the phone." I answer and hear Brother's voice. I know, if he wasn't on the Feds phone, he would have called a hit, but he has to maintain his composure and talk in a civilized manner. I tell him that I'm going to the funeral and that I will do everything I think he would do for the family. He tells me to come see him ASAP, and I know that would be a Thursday evening visit. I hang up the phone and relax for the next day and a half.

When it was time for me to leave, Buddy drives me to the airport, and I try to prepare myself for a devastating funeral.

Chapter Nine

Tony's Frustration

Tonight, went down the way it was supposed to go. At the rate that I'm going, I'll be the king of New York in no time. I got a little injured in the process, but it ain't nothing I can't handle. Niggas need to know who to respect and they need to know who the man is. If they don't know, then I'll have to show them by any means necessary. I'm at a point now where I don't give a fuck and when I get the name of my girl's connect, it will be a wrap. All these sorry-ass niggas gotta come my way, so best believe the stakes will be high. Me and my brothers got a whole lot of shit in store for these cats, so they better get with the program. Time is ticking and this shit is not a game.

As I think about these punk-ass niggas, my arm starts hurting me. Damn I miss my girl and I need her here to take care of me. I wonder what she's doing and if her grandmother is alright. Let me call her and see what's the deal.

Right now, my blood is boiling. I call Tasty and express to her how much I miss and need her but while I'm talking to her, what do I hear? A nigga's voice in the background. She can't tell me I didn't hear a nigga's voice and to top it off, she hangs up on me. I'm so fucking tight right now, I could hurt somebody. I knew she was fucking around. Bitches ain't faithful. Walking around here like she's all innocent while she's fucking on the low. You just wait 'til she gets back. I'm fuck her up for deceiving me. I looked up to that bitch for years and slowly took my time making love to her and this is what I get? Would she love and respect me if I had taken the pussy and fucked it out? Silly girl! I'm tight, real tight. But she will pay for my hurt. Matter of fact, I ain't even gonna fuck with her. I can have any bitch I want; cuter and more fly. Yeah! You see, if she didn't hang up on me, I would have told her about Larry. I bet she'll be all disappointed to know she will miss the funeral. Oh well, fuck her. I should have. Matter of fact. I will! She begged for this dick and NOW she's going to get it. I got a trick for that ass.

Chapter Ten

Acceptance

Yes, it's me, Cee-Cee, in the illest black two-piece Marc Jacobs suit with the bag, shoes and shades to match. Ice in the ears, on the neck, wrists, fingers and ankle. Simple shit but exquisite but, no matter how good I look, hurt and sorrow is written all over my face.

Stacy is here for my support and I'm trying hard to hide my true feelings because Keba is falling apart. Every time I look at her a lump forms in my throat. This is too much to bear. Someone I've known damn near my whole life is laying there, stone cold dead. I mean, what could anyone really say to a wife and two kids who are left behind? Nothing really and nothing helps. I sit here and watch Keba go through the motions of crying, screaming and falling out. My head is hurting. I just wanna run and keep running and leave all this shit behind. If I could run away, I would go back to the Islands. Antigua would be my home with no problems, no worries and no pain. I'll just live life to the fullest, grow old and die. My mind is all over the place right now. I can't breathe or focus. I need air. I gotta go outside. This is too much.

"Stacy, let's go and get some fresh air."

"Are you alright, Cee-Cee?'

"No! I need a cigarette."

"Okay, but the service is gonna start soon."

"We'll be back for it. Let's just go please."

We get up and go outside. It's breezy, but it feels nice. I light my cigarette and take deep, long drags. Yeah, I need this. We sit on two cushioned folding chairs on the veranda and stare into the moonlight. It is peaceful. After I finish my cigarette, I stand up, turn around and walk back towards the door. Suddenly, I stop in my tracks as I hear an all too familiar voice call my name. I turn around and it's Tony. Tony looks sharp as shit, but he is pale in the face. I walk up to him and say, "What's up?" but before I can say another word, I cry my eyes out on his shoulder. He comforts me and dries my eyes. Then we all go inside and take a seat for the funeral service.

The funeral service is long, tearful and heartfelt by everyone in attendance. Even though these people are my people, I can't wait to get out of here. As soon as the service is over, I walk up to Keba and tell her how sorry I am and that Brother sends his love and deepest sympathy. I let her know that I have something special for her and the kids and when she feels up for having company. I make her promise to call me, and I tell her that I'll come right over with what I have for them. I give her a hug followed by a kiss on the cheek and signal to Stacy that we're leaving. Once we get outside in the cool air, I look around and realize I told the limo to come back at nine, and it's only eight o'clock. Damn! We can't just stand out here and there are no cabs around.

"Cee-Cee, what are you doing out here?" Tony asks.

"Tony, I'm leaving. I can't stay any longer. I can't handle things like this."

"I hear that. Well, how are you getting home? Who brought you up here?"

"I hired a limo, but I told the driver to come back at nine. I was just about to call him and let him know that I am ready."

"No need for that, Cee-Cee. I'll take you home. Let me say good-bye to Keba and I'll be right with y'all."

"You don't have to Tony. I think you should stay with Keba. She needs all the support she can get. We'll be fine."

"Listen, I'm gonna say my goodbyes and then I'll take y'all home, ok?"

"Alright," I finally agree.

After Tony disappears, Stacy says, "Girl! Tony is one fine-ass muthafucka. I know you're riding that dick. Just looking at him turns me on. What are you gonna do about C-note?"

"First off, I'm not thinking about that. I'm depressed because a dear friend of mine is laying in a coffin so, the size of Tony's dick, his looks and however he makes you feel is of no concern to me. And second, I would never leave C-note. We are forever. That's it. That's all."

"I'm sorry and you're right. This is not the time for that kind of talk."

As Tony approaches us again, he says, "I'm ready," and escorts us to his brand-new, money-green, Hummer.

I say, "Damn, is this you?"

He smiles and says, "Yeah. Things are looking up."

"I hear that. You better enjoy it while it last 'cause you never know when it'll be your time to go."

"Tasty, I ain't going nowhere."

Stacy says, "Hey, what's this Tasty shit? You got a nickname now?"

"Gurrl, be quiet and relax. Don't get it twisted."

"Well, whatever it is. It sounds delicious to me."

"Ha, ha, ha! Very funny, Stacy. Now, let's just hurry up and drop her off."

We ride out to Queens, smoking crazy weed. We stop at the liquor store and buy two bottles of Moet. When we get in front of Stacy's house, we park the car, roll crazy blunts and drink the Moet from the head. I'm fucked up and so is Stacy but Tony is just chilling. He knows how to control his high. As he is listening to us talk shit, slurring in our words, talking about how we wanna kill those Bronx bitches, he says, "It's time for Stacy to go in and go to bed."

He walks her to her door, makes sure she gets in and returns to the car. Tony starts up the Hummer and we are off on our way uptown. While driving in silence, all I can do is think about Larry. The more I think about him, the more I cry. I'm so fucked up and high right now you would think that would solve my problems and take my hurt away, but it doesn't. I think I feel worse than before.

Pulling up in front of my building is a relief. I can't wait to take off my clothes, brush my teeth, take a nice hot shower and get in my bed. Today has been extremely long and exhausting and I've been on the go since five o'clock this morning. I need to shut it down. My body is aching for rest. After Tony walks me up to my door, I turn around and say, "I need to be alone tonight."

Tony looks at me and says, "Tonight is not a good night for you to be by yourself."

Reluctantly, I agree and let him in. I march straight to the bedroom and perform my nightly ritual. When I get out of the shower and walk back to my room, Tony is sitting up in my bed with just his boxers and wife beater on, rolling a blunt. I notice that he got a surgical pad on his shoulder.

"Oh my God! Tony, what happened to you?"

"Nothing really. I went to a club and got into it with some drunk-ass nigga and he stabbed me in the shoulder."

"Are you alright? Does it hurt? Do you want me to look at it?"

"Nah, it's cool."

"Where's the guy now?"

"Cee-Cee, don't ever ask questions like that."

"Okay. I'll leave it, but don't let this stab wound get infected."

"I won't."

After I finish getting myself ready for bed, I get underneath the blankets, smoke some weed and turn my back towards Tony.

Tony puts the blunt out, dims the lights and says, "What guy did you spend the last couple of days with?"

I turn around to face him and say, "I wasn't with any man."

"So, who was the nigga's voice I heard in the background and why did you hang up on me?"

"I didn't hang up on you. The phone went dead and the guy's voice you heard is a friend of mine from around my grandma's way. Why am I justifying myself to you anyway, Tony?"

"Because you are my fucking woman and I need to know if you are that muthafucking crazy to be with the next nigga."

"I am not your woman. You said, I had one week to think about what I wanted to do and if I'm not mistaken, it hasn't been a week yet but, if you want an answer now, then the answer is no. I can't have you as my man and hurt C-note. No, no, no. It can't go down like that."

"Are you sure?" he asks.

"Yes, I'm sure," I answer.

"So why am I lying next to you naked. Is this how you treat all your friends?"

"Tony, I didn't ask you to get in my bed. I really didn't want you to come in, but since you're here, I said fuck it. It's not like we are going to fuck. So, let's just end this convo, get some sleep and tomorrow get back into business mode. It is better that way."

"Oh so, you wanna get tough? You wanna be Miss Balla-Shot-Caller? Huh! Huh! You think I'm on your shit? Nah baby, but I'ma let you go ahead and sleep that Moet off because this ain't you talking, so we'll end this convo here."

I roll back on my side and in less than no time, I am out like a baby.

Startled by the rings on my phone, I jump up to answer and see that it's a pre-paid call. Before the automated voice finishes, I quickly press five.

"Hello."

"Hey wifey," Cee-note answers.

"I love you," I tell him.

"I love you more. How are you holding up?"

"Baby, this shit is crazy, and you know what? I'm kind of glad you and Brother are in there. I would die if I had to be the one burying one of you guys."

"Nah, you wouldn't be burying us. We don't chase pussy."

"I know that's right."

"So, how is Brother?"

"Fucked up, but I'm going up there to see him on Thursday."

Five minutes into my conversation, Tony rolls over and glides his hand across my neatly shaved Mohawk pussy. I push his hand away and he gives me a look as if to say, "Don't push my hand away." Tony parts my legs and forces his upper body between them and moves his body lower until his face meets my pussy. He slides my thong to the side, takes a deep lick of my sweetness which makes me gasp while holding the phone and trying to push his head away at the same time.

"Cee-Cee, are you listening to me?" C-note asks.

"Yes honey."

"Are you sure you are alright? I don't want you over there dwelling too much on Larry. That's beyond our control and we must move on."

"I know," I say all sexy.

Tony is sucking the shit out of my pussy and while my man thinks I'm crying, I am actually moaning and enjoying this very pleasurable head.

"Cee-Cee."

"Yes…Ooh, baby. I can't talk right now. I feel like I wanna scream."

"I understand wifey. I'll check up on you later. Okay?"

"Mmmh. Ummh."

I don't even say bye, or I love you. I just hang up the phone. I hold on to Tony's head and gyrate on his face. As I get wilder, he rips my thong off and comes up to my face. He opens my legs wider and I wrap my legs around his legs. He rubs his hardness between my lips and grinds on my groin.

"Umm…yeah, Tony."

"You want this, Tasty?"

"Yes, Tony! Put it in!"

"You want all of it?"

"All of it, baby."

"You can't handle all of this."

"Tony, why do you tease me? Stop teasing me and give it to me."

"No, you ain't ready."

Tony grinds on my pelvis showing me he can fuck. He slides his dick up and down on my clit, my pussy gets wetter and wetter and my hole is dying to be entered. Tony sticks his tongue in my mouth and kisses me like I've never been kissed before. Damn…I want him. Why is he tormenting me like this? I don't understand. Tony takes his dick in his hand and rubs the head all over my pussy. My moans become more intense and my legs open wider anticipating his entrance.

"Cee-Cee, you want this big fat dick?"

"Yes Tony."

"Then, tell me what I wanna hear. Tell me, it's all about us, and there's no more C-note. Tell me, Cee-Cee. Tell me!"

"Baby, it's whatever. I want you and I need you now."

"Do you understand what you're saying to me?"

"Yes, Tony yes."

Tony looks down at me with a look I've never seen before. It's so cold, and between gritted teeth, he says, "Don't move. Just feel."

Tony takes the head of his dick, slides it down to my wet, sticky hole and pushes it in. I moan, "Tooooonnnnnyyyy," because the head is unbelievably big and he moans, "Cee-Cee," because my pussy is crazy tight. Tony pushes in more and more until four inches of his python is inside me. Not only is it hurting, but he says, something I can't believe. "Cee-Cee, junior is coming. Don't ever abort my baby or else I will kill you. Feel it Tasty, feel our baby."

Four inches of Tony's dick is inside of me and I can feel it throbbing and shooting out heavy gusts of cum. His eyes are closed and his jaw is tight. He put every drop of his semen inside of me. When he was finished, he brings my legs up to his waist, I wrap my legs around him while his dick was rock hard. He pushes his dick further inside, taking his time until all of it disappears inside of my tightness. As he slowly long-dicks me, I cry. Tears are running down my face because I know this is very dangerous and at the same time, it feels so damn good. Tony works his dick in and out of me slowly, making my pussy loosen up, but my pussy still has a tight grip on him. He knows he must take it easy.

"You like that, Cee-Cee?"

"Yes Tony."

"Cee-Cee, your pussy is so tight and wet. I'm gonna live in here. I'm gonna always sex this sweet, fat pussy. This is mines, all mines. Oh God! Baby! You…feel…so…good."

Tony speeds up the tempo with some short strokes and then long, deep strokes. I feel my body going through some changes.

"Tony, Tony, Tony. This is too much for me. Take it easy."

Tony's mind is gone. It's like he can't hear me and he is steady thrusting his manhood inside of me.

"Fuck me, Cee-Cee."

"I can't. It's too big."

Tony grunts, groans, pants and works his ass up into a frenzy. I unwrap my legs from around his waist and try to push him off me, but I can't budge him. I put my hand between our pelvic areas to slide his dick out and Tony beats the shit out of my hand with his pelvic bone which made him ram me harder.

"Tony, please stop. I can't breathe!"

"I can't Cee-Cee. I gotta cum first. My second nut always takes the longest. I told you…you weren't ready for this. Ahhh! Yeah, Cee-Cee! Your pussy is just how I imagined it would be. I don't wanna stop."

"Oh God! Oh God, I'm gonna cum. Tony."

"Yeah Tasty, cum on my dick. Cum on your man's dick. Soak my dick with all your hot juices. Yeah, yeah, yeah."

Tony brings my legs back up while slamming his dick inside of me. His balls slap and tap against my ass and my pussy walls contract on his dick. I shake and cum so hard that my moans turn into screams of, "Ah! Ah! Tony."

Tony thrusts and thrusts his dick inside of me without mercy. I'm so weak from cumming that I can't take no more. I whisper, "Please, Tony stop."

"Cee-Cee...I love your hot, tight pussy. Don't stop me. Please don't stop me. Let me cum. I'm almost there baby. Oh Tasty, this is the wettest, tightest pussy I have ever been in. Your pussy is sucking my dick so hard. It's driving me crazy. Promise me, baby, that you'll never give my pussy away."

"I promise. I promise. Now cum."

Tony picks up the pace, brings an unbearable amount of pain to my belly and by this time, my pussy is dry. Tony pumps and pumps away and screams, "Yes Tasty, I'm cumin'." He opens my legs wider and like a machine gun, he pumps his body and cums all inside of me. Tony drains his dick to the very last drop and pumps until his dick gets soft. Then, he slowly pulls out and lays on top of me. My legs are so weak and sore that I can hardly move them. My pussy is swollen. It feels like I have a black eye. Tony lays there on top of me and I notice that his bandage is covered in blood.

"Tony get up!" I shout. "Your shoulder is bleeding and you need to change your bandage."

"In a minute. Let me relax."

"Okay, but I need for you to get up so I can go to the bathroom."

Tony rolls off me and it's a struggle for me to walk and urinate. I damn near crawl back to the bed and tell Tony I'm in a lot of pain."

"My vagina is swollen, and it hurts a lot," I say.

Without saying a word, Tony gets up, walks to the bathroom and returns with a cold rag. He opens my legs and lovingly places the rag between my legs. Immediately, it eases the pain and takes down the swelling. As the rag gets warm, Tony takes his hot mouth and puts it on my clit.

"What are you doing, Tony? My shit is swollen?"

"I know, but your pussy looks so good and extra fat that I have to suck it. I'll be gentle. Just relax."

Tony licks me gently. Even though I can't feel it because I am numb as hell, it seems like he is being gentle. All I can see is his head moving up and down and I begin to relax. I am so turned on and loving every minute of it that the pleasure overrides the pain. I grip the back of his head and open my legs wider, so he can soothe my pussy with his tongue.

"Oooh Tony, I love the way you make me feel."

Tony sucks me so good until I cum in his mouth and he drinks every bit of it. When he finishes lapping up my cum, he crawls on top of me and say, "I want some more of you."

I really can't handle the pressure of his dick, but he promises to take it easy this time. Even though he is still excited, he knows my pussy is beat down. It's fragile and needs to be handled with care. Tony rubs his dick on the outside of me. His penis is hard as a brick. He pushes it against my vagina and we both moan. Slowly and gently his dick makes its way through and he slow-motion grinds me. My insides are very tender but the slower he strokes, the wetter and better it feels. It feels so good that I can't help but grind with his rhythm. He moans, "Yeah Tasty. Rock with me. Don't this feel good baby?"

"Yes."

"If you only knew how good you feel, you would always want me to make love to you. I'm gonna make you love me, Cee-Cee."

Tony throws some long strokes with his hips, brings my legs up and dips his stick in my honey. I grab onto his ass and squeeze it as he dips in and out of my pussy. He moves a little faster and I'm riding his rhythm.

"Cee-Cee, your pussy is fucking my head up. I ain't never had anything as tight and sweet as this. Come on baby, fuck this dick. Yeah, like that. Ooooo! Oooooh yeah, Cee-Cee."

As I wind my body from underneath, I feel my body contracting to cum. I squeeze his dick with my pussy muscle, and he screams, "Shit! Shit! Shit! Fuck! Oh God! I'm gonna bust. Oh Cee-Cee. What are you doing to me?"

"I'm gonna cum too."

While we both let off, we scream calling each other's names. This is it. I'm head over heels and seriously in trouble. Tony cuddles me up in his arms and we lay there for hours talking about sex, drugs and his favorite word...OWNERSHIP.

Chapter Eleven

Pleasure Pain

For the last couple of days, Tony and I have been inseparable. We basically stayed in the house and romanced each other. Nothing is really going on and the girls aren't due back until next week, so it's easy to lay up and chill. Tony's gash is healing properly so he'll be ready for business next week. Everything is going according to schedule and things will be back to normal soon. Tomorrow, I'll go see Brother and Saturday I'll see C-note. C-note...what am I gonna do? If he was a woman beater, I sure as hell would be pushing up daises. Still...I'm about to play Russian roulette with my life and this shit ain't funny at all.

Ever since Tony and I made love, my cell has been turned off and the house phone unplugged. Tony says, that he doesn't want no interruptions, so I just left it like that. I enjoy being around Tony. He's funny, lovable, romantic, demanding and loves to fuck. I have never met anyone that can cum six to seven times in a day, and every time we have sex, it's always better than the last time. I know I shouldn't get carried away but I'm feeling him and I want him inside of me until C-note gets home. I'm too caught up to get out now. Besides, he ain't letting me go. He already made it clear that he is playing for keeps. He can have me now, but I'm not leaving C-note. I would never, not in this lifetime. C-note is all the man that I need. I'm just having fun and when the time is right, I'll break it off with Tony. I know it won't be easy and he probably will tell C-note, but I'll tell him first. I'll write Tony a letter and gently let him down. I know he'll be mad, but he'll love me more for my honesty.

Tony left my place early this morning, so I plugged the phone back in the wall and made some calls. The first person I call is my gynecologist. I need an appointment ASAP, so I can get on some sort of contraceptive. Tony is dead set on getting me pregnant and I can't let that happen. I would lose C-note forever behind that shit and that's just being careless. I sure hope I don't get pregnant between now and then. That would be fucked up. I would have to go into hiding.

My second call is to Stacy. She's chilling and wants to roll with me Sunday on some cool out shit. I tell her yeah and that we will have dinner at City Island.

My third call is to Buddy. He tears me a new asshole and says, "Brother and C-note have been calling all around town looking for you and no one knows where you were. Niggas been calling and looking for Tony, and he couldn't be found either, so what the fuck is going on? This morning, Tony was seen and now you're calling."

Before I can respond, my phone beeps. I try to ignore it, but Buddy hears it and says, "Answer deh bloodclatt phone."

I put him on hold and click over. SHIT! It's a pre-paid call from Otisville. Oh no! I press five.

"Are you finish fucking?" C-note shouts.

"I got Buddy on the other line, let me click off."

"Hurry the fuck up!"

I click back to Buddy and tell him, "I gotta go. It's C-note and he's on fire."

"Ah good feh yah rass. If you really ah fuck dat worker, ah dead him dead. Jus mek sure yu call me back. One!"

I click back over to C-note and with a baby voice I say, "Hey baby. Why I got to be fucking? Huh? Since when you got on some paranoid shit? I thought you said that you would never accuse me?"

"Well, ever since your ass went MIA, I have no choice but to believe what I'm hearing."

"Oh yeah! So, my word ain't shit now? Who am I supposed to fucking, C-note?"

"You know who. Don't fucking play games with me. I know Tony's been all up in my pussy for the last couple of days."

"What? What's with this Tony shit? Whoever is watching me needs to mind their fucking business. I don't even feel we should be having this conversation because I ain't fucking anybody."

"Yeah aiight. Bring your ass up here on Thursday."

"I can't. I gotta go see Brother."

"He already knows you're coming up here Thursday, so you'll be seeing him on Saturday. So make sure your ass is here."

"I love you C-note."

"One!"

C-note hangs up on me for the very first time, without saying I love you. This is not good. I don't even want to go up there and see him, but I have too. I'll just keep playing dumb until it blows over. I'm supposed to call Buddy back, but shit…that's gonna have to wait until another time. I'm not in the mood to hear shit. I stretch out and lay on my bed, feeling very exhausted. I decide to make one more phone call and that's to Tony.

After a couple of rings, he picks up and says, "Hey Tasty. I was just thinking about you."

"Oh yeah?"

"Yeah. Did you just get up?"

"Yep, but I'm still tired and I'm going back to bed. I just called to see if you are aiight and if you're thinking about me."

"Tasty, I'm always thinking about you. Did you eat yet?"

"No, I didn't do anything yet. I just made some phone calls and now I'm talking to you."

"Well, get up, get in the shower, put on something sexy and make us some breakfast. I'll be home in twenty minutes."

"You'll be home?"

"Yeah, I'll be home…and Tasty, don't ever starve my baby. I want my son to be real strong."

"Tony, stop with the baby shit. I don't think I can have babies and I don't want you getting disappointed if it doesn't happen."

"My baby is there. I can feel it."

"Aiight. See you in twenty minutes."

"I love…"

Before Tony can finish his sentence, I hang up the phone. I don't want to hear about any love, a baby or anything that is going to cause ruckus in my life. I know he's pissed that I hung up, but hey, I'll just say I didn't hear him.

After coming out of the shower, I put on my peach VS silk negligee that stops mid-thigh with a split on the side and a peach thong. I lotion my body with Channel and gloss my lips with Mac peach lip glass. I put my hair in six flat twists in the front of my head and the rest hangs down the back. I'm just so sexy.

I go to the kitchen and start preparing banana pancakes, scrambled eggs with cheese, home fries, bacon and sausages. While I set the table and prepare the food, my doorbell rings. I answer and it's Tony. He walks in and inhales the sweet aroma of his breakfast.

"That smells good, Tasty. I thought you would be over here burning up shit."

"Boy you crazy. I can cook my ass off. You ain't seen or tasted nothing yet."

"That's what I like. A wife that cooks."

"Yeah, well sit down because it's on the way."

Tony sits in the kitchen area and I wait on him like I'm his waitress. When Tony gets his plate, he is amazed by how everything is so neatly arranged, stacked and plentiful. He eats my fine cooking, licks his fingers and compliments me on the best breakfast he has ever eaten. I can tell he's impressed and that was just breakfast. After eating my food, I get up and clean the kitchen. Tony goes to the living room and puts on some music and rolls a blunt. He blasts the music loud so I can enjoy it too. Tony comes back into the kitchen and stands behind me at the sink. Since my hands are wet from washing the dishes, he holds the blunt up to my lips, so I can get some pulls. I lean the back of my head on his chest and feel the weed flow through my system. While this is happening, Tony caresses my stomach and rubs his hard dick against my ass. I grind on it, letting him know that I acknowledge his erection. He moves his hands down between my legs and rubs my pussy through my silk thong. My clit is getting erect and my cream is soaking the thong material. I open my legs wider, so he can get a better play and he plays in my pussy. First, he is dead set on playing with my clit, then he rubs the whole pussy and finally he fingers fucks me with two fingers. After he brings me to my first orgasm for the day, I thought he would let me finish cleaning the kitchen, but instead, he runs tiny little kisses down my back to the crack of my ass. He slightly bends me over, kisses and caresses my ass cheeks. While he's on his knees, he spreads my ass cheeks and sticks his hot, long tongue in my pussy. He eats my pussy from the back and slides his tongue up and down the crease of my ass. Tony stands up on his feet again, pulls his shirt over his head, drops his jeans and boxers to his ankles, and pushes his big, fat mushroom dick head inside of me. I grab on to the sink and moan with pleasure as he strokes that pipe in and out ever so gently.

"Ooooh Tony."

"Yes, baby?'

"I don't want you to ever stop."

"I won't. This is my pussy. You belong to me."

Tony pulls the back of my hair and brings my upper body to meet his and shoves his watery, pussy-flavored tongue down my throat. While he's tonguing me and pumping his hot meat inside of me, he reaches for my clit and goes crazy on it. I moan louder in his mouth, and for the first time, I tell him, "Fuck me harder! Give me all you got and make me cry." Screaming all the fuck talk turned Tony on so much that he bends me over to whereas I am holding my ankles, grabs my waist and long dicks me. That shit feels so good that I feel like I am losing my mind.

Tony is behind me putting some serious back motion into it. He slaps my butt, spreads my ass cheeks and moans in ecstasy, "Tasty! You make me feel so good. I love the way your tight pussy sucks my dick. You've got the creamiest pussy I've ever seen, tasted or been in."

I know he is hooked, and so am I. Tony continuously fucks the shit out of me, and I can feel his dick growing more and more. I bounce back on his dick feeling all ten inches of his fat meat inside my guts, killing me softly and I don't tell him to stop. I am zoning and this is feeling so fucking good. Tony speeds up the pace a bit more and thrusts hard, shouting out he's about to cum and beats my pussy up with his dick, stirs his cock in all different directions and put loads of hot cum in my stomach. Standing in a gentle embrace, I felt that it was meant to be. We are in the moment. I kiss him gently, pull away and walk to the bathroom to wash up.

After getting dressed and cleaning up, I sit next to Tony, relax and surf the TV for something good to watch. I rest my head on his shoulder, turn to him and say, "Tony, I'm going to see C-note tomorrow." Tony grabs me by the neck, pulls me off the couch, and slams me up against the wall. I am so scared, crying, can't breathe and completely speechless.

"T...T...Tony. Get off me. What are you doing?" I finally say.

"What am I doing? You're carrying my fucking child and telling me you're going to see your ex?"

"But Tony! He's not my ex. You know I just can't get up and walk out of C-note's life like that, and I'm not pregnant."

"Cee-Cee, do you wanna die right now? I'll snap your fucking neck if you continue talking that crazy shit."

"What shit, Tony?"

"What did you say? What did you beg me to do a couple of days ago. Didn't I tell you that you weren't ready? Huh! Huh! You think I'm a fucking joke?"

Tony slaps the shit out me real hard knocking me to the floor. I try to get up and run, but he grabs me by the back of my hair and drags me to the bedroom. My mind is gone. No man has ever hit me and now I'm getting fucked up. Tony swings me on the bed, jumps on top of me and continues to slap me all up in my face. Within seconds, my face is sore, bruise and swollen. When Tony finish punishing my face, he drags me to the shower, washes me and himself. I am so shocked, hurt and disgusted, I don't know what to do. When we got out of the shower, he dried me off, picked out some nightwear, put me in it and told me to get in the bed. Tony unplugs the house phone again, gets dressed, walks over to my bag, takes my house keys and says, "I'll be back."

When Tony left my apartment, I cry hysterically and run to the mirror to look at my face. I can't believe this is me in the mirror. My face is swollen with red handprints. I cry and cry some more. What am I gonna do? I can't see C-note and Brother looking like this. They will order a hit. I don't want anyone's blood on my hands. Oh God! Help me, I pray. This is all my fault. Why did I sleep with him? It's too late to turn back the clock and way too late for *should of, could of, would of*. So, in order to not get killed, I can't talk about C-note. I'll let Tony think it's over between me and C-note and play the part until C-note gets home. But, I make up my mind that Tony will pay for this shit. I promise. As for tomorrow, I'll tell C-note that the car broke down and that I'll see him next week. I love him and I'll never let him go.

I walk to the kitchen and fill a bucket with ice. I take it into the bedroom where I keep putting ice on my towel to take down the swelling on my face. Not only is my face achy, but my body is too. Since I can't go outside or use any of my phones, I'll try to focus on something else like dinner. It's still early so I'll take out some steaks to thaw, lay down and relax until five.

"Cee-Cee. Cee-Cee." Tony nudged Cee-Cee's arm.

"Yeah, what time is it?"

"It's eight o'clock. Wake up. I need to talk to you."

"What Tony? I'm tired and my face and neck is sore."

"Baby, I'm so sorry. I can't believe I acted like that. Never in a million years, would I have ever imagined putting my hands on you. I don't know what got into me and I'm very sorry."

"Tony, you hurt me. You hurt me in a way that no man ever has before, and I don't know how to forgive you. Look at my face Tony. I look like a monster. This is what your so-called love did. Is this how it's going to be? Because if so, then there are plenty of naturally ugly girls out there you can have, own or whatever."

"I understand all that and there's no excuse for my behavior. I drove around all day, hating myself for hurting someone I truly love. I love you Tasty, and I wanna be with you, but I gotta say this. I can't have you talking about or seeing C-note. Your relationship with him ended when we made love. When I bedded you, it was without a condom. You got all of me. I made love to you, Tasty. I know I can get out of hand and be a little rough, but that's only because it's flesh on flesh and I am enjoying myself giving you all of me. I love the way you make me feel. I love how you feel inside and out. This is what I've been wanting for the last three years and now that I got you, I will never let you go. Do you understand what I'm saying?"

"Tony, I understand what you're saying, but when you met me, I was with someone. I've been with this person damn near all my life. I love him unconditionally and it's hard for me to let go. In order for me to love you one hundred percent, you got to let me do what I got to do. Let me pull away from him on my own. Let me drop out of love because, if you're doing everything right, then you don't have anything to worry about. You got the advantage right now, so me going to visit him. Sending him money and talking to him can't hurt anything. I don't have a problem telling C-note that it's over but let me do it face to face. I owe him that much respect. Please?"

"That's why I love you. Yeah, go up there next week and handle your business, because after that I need to be secure with my feelings. I need to know that I have you all to myself. I'm stuck, head over heels and loving you hard. You are going to be my wife and the mother of my child. That I promise. Were you gonna cook tonight?"

"Yeah, I wanted to make some grilled T-bone steaks, baked potatoes and steamed broccoli."

"Well, you get some rest, and I'll make it."

"What? You can cook?"

"I won't say anything. I'll let you be the judge. I love you Tasty, and I'll do anything for you."

After kissing me gently on the lips and forehead, Tony disappears into the kitchen. I lay back down and thank God for that golden opportunity to see C-note. Next Thursday, I will be on a mission.

Chapter Twelve

C-note's Frustration

I can't believe I've been calling my girl for the past couple of days and she hasn't been answering her phones. I'm so frustrated that I don't know what to do with myself. I need to get in touch with her to let her know that she needs to see me on Thursday.

Things are getting real serious and we need to talk about our relationship. I know she's fucking around with Tony. I'm pissed about it but, fo-real, fo-real, what can I do about it? I just want her to know to be careful and take care of business. I'll never leave her even if my heart is broken. I got to let Cee-Cee be Cee-Cee. She's a smart girl and I know she'd never put herself in a situation that she can't handle.

Tony played himself big time. I'm going to crush his skull. Of all people, he should know better. If Cee-Cee was fucking somebody else, I wouldn't be so upset, but this punk-ass nigga keeps disrespecting the game. I have no choice but to put all the blame on him. I know it takes two to tango, but my girl is vulnerable and I'm sure he took advantage of her. One year left and he does this dumb shit. Yo! Just the thought of his ass making love to my woman got me on fire. Knowing his ass, he is probably stopping Cee-Cee from answering the phone, but she should know better. She is a businesswoman. Her phone must stay on. No dick on earth is that good to make her neglect her obligations. She is getting beside herself. I'm a walk my ass over to the phone and call her again. It's bad enough she has me and Brother calling all over the place for her. I'm worried. I can just imagine how Brother and Buddy feel. Well, I'll try again in a few.

I just got off the phone with Cee-Cee. Finally, her ass picked up. She wants to act like she doesn't know what the fuck I'm talking about. She says that everybody is lying. I'm more than pissed. How the fuck is she gonna lie to me? Yeah, I'm gonna be mad, but what the fuck? Lying is what's going to destroy our relationship. I can't wait for her to come up here. Whether she likes it or not, she is going to confess to me. I need to know what is really good. Right now, I'm gonna get some sleep and when I wake up, it should be time for my visit.

Ah Thursday! Let me get ready for my visit. I'll go shower, put my neatly-ironed uniform on with that cheap ass Calvin Klein oil they sell in commissary and wait patiently for my name to be called. It is twelve noon and no Cee-Cee. *Did she get into an accident?* I thought. I call, call and call. No answer. I say to myself she must have a damn good explanation for this. This is the first time she has ever missed a visit. I hope she's alright. I'll try to call her later.

After days of trying to reach Cee-Cee, I go to the priest at the chapel and make a sacred deal with him. I knew someone would want this paper, and it just so happens to be the priest. I explain to him what is going on with me and Cee-Cee and he understands. We make a deal for a private, one-on-one visit for three hours and he'll get paid three geez. I tell him how he will get the money, and he loves it. I explain to him that I don't know when she'll be coming, but whenever she does, he needs to get her and pull her name. We shake on it and I bounce.

Now, all I got to do is wait for Cee-Cee to come. I'm not going to spaz on her. I'm trying to be as rational and civilized as I can, but we will establish a lot of things and I'll know where we stand.

Chapter Thirteen

Confession

Today is going to be the longest, scariest and most heart-breaking day of my life. I sit here in the waiting area at Otisville, and my heart begins to pound like crazy, and I can hear it. Tears begin to well up in my eyes and I just don't know what to do. First, I'm mad because my gynecologist says I couldn't get on any contraceptives until after my menstrual cycle and that's not until another two weeks from now. I am destined to get pregnant if have to keep having sex all day, everyday with Tony.

Second, I gotta sit down and tell C-note what is really going on. I really wanted to explain it in a letter but I owe him at least this much face-to-face. While I'm sitting here having crazy thoughts and fighting my anxiety, a priest comes up to me and calls my name. I look up and say, "Yes, that's me. Is there something wrong?"

"There's nothing wrong young lady. I'm going to walk you through security and you're going to follow me. Your visit will be held in the Chaplain's office today, not in the visiting room," the priest answers.

"Why? What happened? Is everything alright with my fiancé?"

"Yes. Yes. This is a special three-hour visit. We only allow three hours because it's a personal visit, so we have to keep it within the correct time frame."

"I understand."

As we pass through security, my heart beats faster and faster. I know I have no choice but to tell C-note now. I just wish we weren't going to be alone.

The priest and I walk down a long-ass hallway and when we pass the chapel, my knees become wobbly. When we get in front of the priest's office, he opens the door and C-note is already there waiting for me. The priest says, "Keep it low and remember you only have three hours."

When the priest turns to leaves, he shuts the door and locks us in. C-note runs over to me. He hugs and kisses me endlessly. I can't breathe but I don't care because, for the first time in three years, I am alone with my man. C-note kisses all over my face and neck while he unbuttons my dress. I'm wearing a fitted denim Versace dress and four-inch, open-toe stilettos. Simple but elegant diamonds adorn my neck, wrist and ears. And of course, I am wearing my twenty-karat, princess-cut, diamond engagement ring. My hair looks tight with a big braid in the back that leans to the side. I am looking every bit of one hundred grand, but I'm not happy.

As C-note finishes unbuttoning my dress, he takes it off my shoulder and lets it drop to the floor. He takes two steps back to observe my body and says, "Cee-Cee, you are fine as hell. Are you ready to make our baby?" Before I have a chance to respond, C-note comes towards me, feeling all over my body and sucking on my breasts. Damn, my man feels good. Now that my body has relaxed, I help him out of his clothes. When all our clothes are off, he walks over to the chair, sits on it and says, "Ride me." I straddle him, put his dick in my hand and guide it into my pussy. I squeeze my pussy muscles real tight, so it fits his dick like a glove. As I put it in, C-note moans with excitement and I moan along with him. While my pussy tightly grabs his dick all the way down, C-note squeezes my fat ass and says, "Yeah mommy. Ride your dick. Show me how much you miss me." I ride my dick like a cowgirl, bucking, thrusting and bouncing crazy on it, not realizing how I'm showing him how experience I've become. I slow-motion grind and fast Calypso wine on it. I do a whole lot more than I use to do with him and with a whole lot less screaming. While I'm fucking my man like the professional I've become, C-note moans and work himself into a frenzy. I damn near have him speaking in tongues. He is slobbering and trying to control my waist, but he can't. He calls my name like a little bitch. I have him for the first time telling me to slow down. "Ooooh mommy, you're fucking the shit out of my dick. Oh God! I don't wanna cum yet. Mommy don't move," he begs. I tic-tock and pop my coochie on his ass and he cries out in pleasure before he shoots his hot milk inside me. C-note holds me tightly and drains himself. As he eases up off of me, I can feel a sense of trouble. I practically told on myself because I have never fucked that way before. So, to take the tension off of me, I begin to suck on his neck. I stick my tongue in his ears and mouth. I get up off him and get on my knees. While his dick is still semi-hard, I hold it, jerk it a little and then kiss it. C-note loves to get his dick sucked and he knows I give incredible head. I can deep throat. I take the tip of my tongue and lick all over his cock. It tastes so good. It's a combination of me, him and Tony. I can actually smell Tony on C-note's dick. As I lick my man's dick, he spreads his legs and leans his head back and says, "Umm…mommy. I miss this. Suck your dick. Yeah baby, suck it."

In one gulp, I swallow his cock. I jerk it in the back of my throat and pull it out, slowly flicking my tongue on the head. His dick instantly gets hard again. As I bob my head up and down, his chest begins to heave. C-note holds the back of my head and fucks my mouth as his dick glides so smoothly down my mouth that it tickled. His moans increase as he gyrates on my face. C-note removes his dick out of my mouth, stands me up and bends me over the little table and pushes his big, hard dick inside of me. He fucks me, putting his back into it. I bounce back heavily, showing him that I can handle whatever he can put out. I put one leg up on the table and tell him to fuck me harder. He pumps and pumps for dear life, sweating like crazy. I pull his dick out of me and lay on the table and put my legs on his shoulder. C-note plunges his dick hard and deep inside of me and calls out my name. C-note spreads my legs wider, digs all up in my belly and plays with my clit. We both scream in ecstasy and cum like crazy.

As soon as we finish recuperating, we go into the priest's bathroom and clean ourselves. We get dressed, sit at the table and stare at each other. My heart is beating rapidly, not because of our sexual act but because of a conversation I didn't want to have.

"Cee-Cee, we need to talk," he says.

"I know, C-note," I answer nervously.

"Do you wanna go first or shall I?"

"You go first, and whatever you hear, don't shout and don't hit me."

"Hit you? I would never put my hands on you. I love you too much to hurt you."

"Okay, so I'm ready."

"Cee-Cee, are you fucking Tony?"

"Damn C-note, why that got to be the first question?"

"Because that would explain why you performed the why you did."

"If I say yes, would you hate me?"

"Just answer the question."

"Yes."

"Have you been using protection?"

"No."

"No!?! So, you could be pregnant and if you are, you wouldn't know who the father is."

"I'm not pregnant and let's not think so far ahead."

"How long has this been going on?"

"Since Larry's funeral, but we've been having foreplay for a while."

"You went down on him?"

"Do you really want me to answer that?"

"Whatever I ask you, I want you to answer."

"Yes, but…"

"No buts, let me ask you this, Cee-Cee? Does he know where we live? How about our connect and the vault?"

"Baby, I will die with that information. I know I am stupid for going to bed with him, but I'm not stupid enough to bankrupt us. C-note, I fucked up. I am so sorry. I can't say that it wasn't my fault, but I did not come on to him. I was so high and drunk, I needed to lay down. When Tony got me to the room, I didn't know he had booked us in together. During that time, he went down on me. I was upset and furious, but what could I do. I was vulnerable. I hated myself afterwards, but then my mind started playing with me. I guess it was because I hadn't been touched by a man in such a long time. His aggressiveness intrigued me and he kept teasing me. He played me. He made me want him sexually and I did. I just wanted to be held and made love to, and when it happened, I got carried away. Tony made me promise that I would leave you. I'm supposed to break up with you today. This is what he wants. Last week, when I told him I was coming to see you, he beat the shit out of me," I confess.

"What? This muthafucka hit you? Cee-Cee, you are fucking my

head up right now. Please tell me you are lying. I'm going to kill him. He is one dead muthafucka. I'm a order a hit from in here. You gotta get away from him."

"No! C-note, don't do it. I'm scared. I cry each and every day behind this, and it's tearing me apart. I don't know what to do."

"Do you love me Cee-Cee?"

"Yes! Of course, I do, with all my heart. I'll never stop loving you. You are my life. I can't live without you. I am so sorry for this mess, but don't put blood on my hands. When you come home, you can deal with it. Tony is determined to stop us from being together and we have to pretend that's the way it is. I know you are upset and ready to kill, but you gotta let me handle my end. I'm the one that's out here. He already told me, if I run away, he will find me, and it won't be a nice situation. All I'm asking is for you to hold your head and hurry up and get home. I won't feel safe until you are there."

As I cry bitterly in C-note's arms, I feel streams of tears run down my neck. C-notes is crying along with me. I know he is hurt, but he knows what I'm saying is true and he doesn't want to endanger my life.

"Baby, I'm a carry on the business just like normal," I reassure him. Everything is still the same. We just got to let him think that it's over between us. I'm going to send you a number where you can call me. I don't want you to call the apartment. I'll see you when I can. I think he has somebody watching me, but I'm not sure. You're camp status now, and so is Brother. It's time for y'all to go there so y'all can get furloughs and handle my problem."

"Cee-Cee, am I supposed to sit back and be okay with Tony having my woman? Not only is he having my woman, but he got my woman so afraid of him that she's ending our relationship? How am I supposed to sleep at night wondering if he's beating the shit out of you? What kind of man do you think I am? You, of all people should know that I can't let that happen. I'm being punked in the worst way one year before my release date. This shit don't look good, but for your sake, I'll back off, but the day I get out, game over."

C-note cradles me in his arms and holds me tight. We have an hour before our visiting time ends. After we converse a bit more, we come to an understanding about the Tony situation and we kiss endlessly.

"Cee-Cee, we got forty-five minutes left. I wanna make love to you and put my baby inside of you. If your period doesn't come, have the baby."

"What? What if the baby belongs to Tony?

"Princess, it doesn't matter because he is a dead man anyway and your baby is my baby. So, lets make love and see if I can get lucky."

C-note undresses himself with his fine ass. He strips all the way down to nothing and then unbuttons me again. We lay the clothes out on the floor and C-note lays on top of them. He tells me to put my pussy in his mouth while I suck his dick. C-note loves the sixty-nine position and so do I. After we suck each other and bring each other to an orgasm, C-note lays me flat on my back, puts my legs on his shoulder and goes to work on me. This is what I love about C-note. No matter how many times he nuts, he can keep a hard-ass dick. While he puts it down on me and shows me who the man is, I cry out in love, pain and pleasure, "I love you! I love you! I love you." C-note thrusts himself hard and deep and calls out my name while cumming frantically inside of me.

After getting dressed, we sit at the table like angels. The priest unlocks the door and says, "Time is up." C-note and I look at each other, hug and kiss everlastingly.

"I love you Cee-Cee," C-note says.

"I love you too," I cry.

As I leave him, I feel exhausted and empty, all I can do is cry. The visit ends exactly three hours after it started, much shorter than the regular visit, but to be honest, it was well worth it. I enjoyed being honest, and I enjoyed making love to C-note. I hope I'm pregnant and I hope the baby is his. But, either way it goes, if I am pregnant, this is C-note's baby and he will be the only daddy my baby will ever know.

Chapter Fourteen

C-note

I feel like shit as I leave the chaplain's office. I am heartbroken and distraught. My woman is out there with this maniac beating on her. I'm going to kill him. I'm going to break him the fuck down. Nobody messes with my woman, my family or my money. He's violated one hundred percent and he's got to pay. This is something I want to handle myself because this needs special attention. I don't even want Brother to get involved, but knowing Brother, I'm sure he will. When Tony put his hands-on Cee-Cee, he put his hands on a lot of people.

It's eight o'clock. I wonder if she made it home alright. Today was really intense for her. I guess the only reason I didn't spaz out is because I already knew. Cee-Cee having sex with another man couldn't tear us apart. That's normal for a woman in her position. I'm glad she held it down for as long as she has. That's why this can't destroy us. Her honesty and love for me is what is keeping us alive, and I got to be strong for her current situation. I love my girl, and I know her heart belongs to me only. I'm a give her a call to let her know I understand.

I can't believe this lowlife muthafucka got the nerve to be answering Cee-Cee's phone. Who the fuck he thinks he is? The only reason I didn't tell him what I really thought about his ass was because I was on the Fed's phone. I really wish I could snap his fucking neck. Tomorrow, I'm gonna put in for camp and get my furlough. Then it's a wrap. I'm going to torture him and make sure he feels every moment of excruciating pain. That I promise.

Chapter Fifteen

Tony's Hype

I can't wait for Cee-Cee to get back. I know she is going to be depressed but I got two beautiful surprises for her. She's going to love them. Hopefully, this will cheer her up. What she went to do today was a very courageous thing. I commend her on her actions but it doesn't make sense to hang on to somebody who doesn't really care for her. C-note doesn't love her. I'm sure he's got a wife and kid somewhere. I bet they are chilling, playing the part and spending the money that she makes, but all that shit stops today and whatever he's got, he can live off of it. Cee-Cee ain't working no more. She's gonna give me that connect and then it's a wrap. All I want her to do is be my wife and have my kids. We deserve each other. I know I can make her feel way better than C-note.

When I make love to her, I put her in a different hemisphere, and she loves that. I'm the second man she's been with and her pussy was made for me. I tapped that ass while it was three years in preserve, and I waited patiently.

C-note must be gutted right now, but I'm the man and by the time he gets out, she'll either have had my baby or be just about to. I love this woman and I'm not letting her go. Besides, with all the things that are going on in my life, I need her connect to make it complete. She is the last piece to my puzzle. It's my destiny to own her and New York.

While waiting anxiously for her to come home, I realize it's nine o'clock. Where the fuck is she? I know her visit with C-note ended at three, so she should have been here at least by five. If this bitch ran off and left me, I will hunt her ass down and she will regret that shit.

Nah! Let me stop. She ain't leaving me. I hope she's aiight and didn't get into an accident. I'm a call her cell.

I ring Cee-Cee's cell and she's not answering. It went straight to voicemail. I am mad as shit. Where could she be? One thing for sure, she better not fuck up my night and she better have a good explanation for coming home late. I know she's going through something but, hey those are the breaks.

Ring! Ring! Ring! The house phone goes off. I answer it, and it's a pre-paid call from C-note. Isn't this a bitch. I press five and say, "What's up son?"

"Yo, who dis?"

"You know who dis is nigga. Only one nigga can answer this phone."

"Yeah...you got a lot of shit with you."

"Nah partner. I'm just being the man that I am."

"Oh yeah! Not for long."

"Nigga, I'm in control. I run the streets. I took your woman and soon she will be having my baby."

"Well, how does it feel to try to be me nigga? You are a lame-ass wannabe. You can't have my woman. All you're doing is keeping my side of the bed warm. Cee-Cee is mine nigga, and I'm coming home to get mine."

"Ha, ha, ha...all that funky fly shit sounds good, so I'm waiting and when come, I'll introduce you to my little friend."

"You ain't ready for that. So, sleep nigga."

"Hey, bitch-ass! You ain't allowed to call this house no more. In fact, after tonight, Cee-Cee won't be living here."

"Click!" I hang up on that asshole. I have no time for bullshit. If he wants some, he can get a whole body full.

Now, where the fuck is Cee-Cee? I'm really getting mad and she doesn't want me to get upset tonight. I don't wanna put my hands on her, but she's forcing me to.

I walk into the bedroom, take out her suitcase and pack all her shit. By the time I was finished, Cee-Cee has five large Louis Vuitton suitcases packed. Damn, she is clothes crazy and they are all expensive. Some still have the price tags on them. I also pack three boxes of shoes and three boxes of bags and hats. She has every flavor leather jacket, two furs and a nice jewelry box. She also has a money machine and couple of duffle bags of lingerie. This girl is unbelievable, but she's fly. I take all these things downstairs to my Hummer and come back and wait patiently for her to come. It's now twelve midnight and I'm going to kill this bitch.

Chapter Sixteen

This Can't Be Happening

I drive as slow as possible, taking my time to get back into the city. I meditate on every reason why I love C-note. If he was somebody else, he would have left me so I consider myself blessed. Today was the worst day of C-note's life and mine as well. I'm sorry it went down like that but I had no choice but to confess. He sensed it anyway and Pete kept him well informed. It's all good now. At least, everything is out in the open. I hate to hide things from him, especially since he's in a place like that, but it is what it is. I will always love C-note and I pray that I am carrying his child. That would be a dream come true.

After pulling up in front of Pete's house, I blow my horn. This good-for-nothing piece of shit sticks his head out of the window and shouts, "I'll be down in a minute." I park the car and chill until he comes down.

Pete is a short dude, well-built and fly as shit. Not my taste but I guess that's why he's hating right now. I bet he would love to be all up inside my tight pussy, but I think not. As he approaches my car, he says, "You're really showing your ass, driving Tony's shit."

"Mind your fucking business. I don't work for you. You work for me so don't tell me shit."

"No girl, you got it fucked up. I work for Brother and C-note."

"Yeah, whatever! But like I said, mind your fucking business. Now, where are we fucking going, snitch?"

"Girl, you better watch you mouth. Don't ever call me a snitch. You think I wasn't going to tell my boss you're fucking on him? Everybody knows."

"And so, what Pete? I confessed to him today, and he knows everything so, you don't have to be his informant anymore."

"Cee-Cee, just drive to the Hilton at JFK Airport and when we get there, park and sit your hot ass in the car and wait."

We ride to the airport in silence. Ever so often, I light up a stogie, smoke some and then put the rest out. I don't know but for some reason, my nerves are bad. I got C-note out of the way early, so I'm not nervous about that. I just hope this girl made it through. I don't want no arrests on my side and if she does get popped, I pray she doesn't give us up. Fo-real, fo-real. I don't need the Feds on my ass.

As I panic for the first time, I begin to feel sick. We pull up into the parking lot, I park and lean the seat back. I reach into my bag and give Pete the girl's pay which is three gees. He gets out and I relax. I'm so relaxed that I fall into a deep sleep.

Waking up four hours later, I bug the fuck out. Am I still at the Hilton waiting for Pete to come downstairs? It's 9:30 pm. I'm hungry, tired and uptight. What the fuck is going on? I take out my cell and call Pete but he doesn't answer. I think to myself, *I'll give this nigga 'til eleven and if he doesn't call, then I'm a leave.* I get out of the car and go into the Hilton. I see they have a little restaurant so I sit and order a meal.

I'm not ordering anything fancy, just a well-done T-bone steak, baked potato and a virgin strawberry Daiquiri. By the time I finish eating, it's 11:20pm. I pay for my dinner, give a nice tip and head back to the car. While approaching the car, who do I see looking mad as shit? Pete. As I come face-to-face with him, I get scared so, in a shaky voice, I ask, "Is everything alright?"

"Where the fuck did you go? Didn't I tell you to sit in the car and wait?" Pete complains.

"I'm gonna ask you again. Did everything go down alright?"

"Of course, it did but where the fuck was you?"

"Now that I know everything went smooth. Why the fuck did you leave me in the car for so many hours? You didn't call, I was hungry and not to mention worried."

"If you would have had your phone turned on, you would have known the plane was delayed. I sat inside the airport all that time. When she came through, I brought her here, got the package, gave her some dick and paid her."

"That's what really took your ass so long? You were upstairs fucking? How dare you fuck these girls while I'm waiting on you! You ain't shit nigga. Put the packages in the back and let me drop you off."

It's 12:30 am and I'm finally getting home. I notice that Tony's Hummer is here so that tells me he is upstairs. I park across the street, adjacent to him and grab the package from the back seat. I lock the car and march my tired ass to my door. I take my keys out of my bag, stick it in the chamber but as soon as I unlock the door and step inside, I receive a hard-ass slap across my face that drops me to my knees. I am so dazed that my vision is blurred. I turn around, look up and see Tony locking the door. I say, "What the fuck did I tell you about putting your hands on me?" Tony reaches down, drags me to my feet, tears my clothes off and beats me up in the worst way.

Every time he slaps and punches me, he calls me a whore. I am so fucked up that I don't know what is going on. All I know is my face is bleeding. I cry and scream for Tony to stop but he will not listen. He just keeps beating me in my face and head until I pass out.

It's five o'clock in the morning. When I wake up, I thank God for bringing me out of this nightmare. I turn over on my side and see Tony laying there, knocked the fuck out, butt ass naked. As I try to get up, my head throbs. I reach to touch it and the pain sends chills up my spine. I try to talk, but my voice is hoarse and my face is tight. "What's is going on?" I whisper. "Am I alright?" I tap Tony lightly on his back. At first, he does not respond, but then he turns around slowly and faces me.

"Tony, I don't feel good. I need some pain killers and help to the bathroom."

Tony looks at me dumbfounded.

"Tony, what's wrong with me?" I ask.

"Cee-Cee, we got into a nasty fight last night."

"What? So, I wasn't dreaming?" I ask, confused.

"I love you Cee-Cee and I'm sorry," Tony apologizes.

"Oh God Tony! What did you do to me? I can't move and I can hardly see."

While tears pour down my eyes, I try not to cry. Tony stands up, picks me up and carries me to the bathroom. After using the toilet, Tony helps me to the sink. When I look up and see my face in the mirror, I bawl and scream loudly. My screams echo throughout the apartment. I stand there horrified, not believing what I am seeing. I have handprints, ring prints, bruises, swollen lips and blood in my braids.

"This is not me! This is not me!" I scream. "Oh God Tony, why did you do this to me?"

Tony stands behind me, holding me up and trying to console me, but I don't want his touch. I just want him to leave.

"Leave Tony! Please get out! Don't come back! I can't live like this. Please leave."

Tony picks me up, put me back in the bed and watches me cry until I fall asleep.

Hours later, I wake up due to the pounding in my head. I painfully try to open my eyes and from what little I can see, Tony is on top of me. He has my knees in his chest and he is trying to force his dick into my pussy.

"No! No! No! Stop!" I cry.

"I'm sorry Cee-Cee. I love you. Please let me love you. I promise this won't ever happen again."

"I don't want you anymore and you're hurting me. I'm dry and you're blistering me. Please stop and get out!"

"Oh Cee-Cee! Your pussy is the best, even when it's dry. I can't stop and I can't leave, baby. Shhh…let me handle this."

Tony pumps and pumps, moaning my name and telling me how much he loves me but at this point, I can't stand him. I hate him and he's hurting me. Tony goes berserk inside of me until he works himself up into a frenzy and cums. My legs are so sore from all the pounding and I can't breathe, see or talk. After Tony is done, he lays on top of me, breathing heavy. I'm fucked up and helpless. He rolls off me, kisses my stomach and says, "We are connected for life."

I close my eyes and sob some more. Tony gets up, takes a shower and then fixes us some breakfast. He comes back and carries all the food on a tray. I am so disgusted that I can't eat. Tony tries feeding me but I can't chew. My jaw and face hurt so much. The pain is overwhelming. I still can't understand why I was beaten up like this.

"Tony, what happened last night? What made you so evil and violent? Do you see what I look like?"

"Tasty, let's just forget about what happened and move on. I got two beautiful surprises for you and later you'll see them."

"Tony, I got a business to run. I can't up and leave when things are coming to me. At six o'clock, I'm supposed to meet someone and I can't go looking like this. They'll be ready to kill you. I need to know why you did this to me?"

"I was mad Cee-Cee. I waited here for you all evening and you never showed up. I called your phone several times and you had the damn thing off. Then, C-note punk ass called."

"C-note called?"

"Yes, that bitch-ass nigga called, and we exchanged words. I had to let him know who the man around here is."

"Why did you have to go there? But that would have to be you, right?"

"Well, just in case you didn't tell him, I had to let him know. So, after I hung up on him, I waited and waited, and you still never came home. All types of shit were going on in my head. I even packed all your things and put them in the Hummer."

"Why did you pack my things?"

"It's a surprise and you'll see tonight."

"Tony, I can't roll with you tonight. I have some business to take care of. The same shit I did last night is the same shit I'll be doing tonight and all week, so you might as well kill me because I gotta go."

"What you gotta do that's so important?"

"Go and look in the living room and find the packages you knocked out of my hand."

Tony gets up and goes to the living room and picks up the neatly packed kilos.

"What is this?" he asks.

"It's six kilos. Business, work and product. This is the shit you've been stressing me about and then damn near kill me over. This is what I was doing while you were thinking I was out there fucking some nigga. You damaged me for no reason."

"So why didn't you tell me what you were doing?"

"Because I couldn't. These people don't play games. They don't want anybody in their fucking business."

"Well let me come with you tonight so you can introduce me to them. We can let them know that I'm your man and that they need to be dealing with me."

"Oh, hell no! We would be shot on the spot. What are you

thinking, Tony? This is not a game or some bullshit TV series. This is real life. I'm going by myself and as long as I'm in this business, I handle this by myself. All you need to do is keep doing what you're doing, and we will stay healthy and alive. We can get large. Just play your position."

"Cee-Cee, I need to meet these people that you deal with. I need your connect."

"What? You can't have my connect. That's my bread and butter."

"I'm not trying to take your shit. I just want to step up the work. That's all. So, instead of shooting me down, just ask them."

"I'll ask them after I turn the heat down on the situation about my face. They are not going to have any understanding of this. I have to come up with some shit to tell them."

"Damn Tasty! If I would have known what you were doing, I would have never done this. You got to open up to me. I'm sorry baby. I'm gonna get this off right now, and I'll be right back. Please don't leave."

"I don't think I can move fast enough."

Tony gets up, get dress and bounce. I pick up the phone and call Pete to find out what time he wants to me to pick him up. He tells me to scoop him up at nine. So, that gives me enough time to rest and pile mad make-up on my face. Pete will have a field day if he sees me tore up like this.

Two hours pass and Tony comes back with the money, a dozen roses and a small box. He puts the money in the closet, lays the roses next to me and tells me to open the box. I unwrap the box and open it and I can't believe my eyes. It's a three Karat diamond platinum engagement ring. I say, "Tony, what is this?"

"Cee-Cee, I want to apologize for last night and for the first time I put my hands on you. I know that I've been a complete jerk. I don't deserve to be in your presence right now, but I can assure you that this type of behavior will never happen again. I love you Cee-Cee, and I will die trying to make you happy. So, today I'm on my bended knee asking for your hand in marriage."

"Tony, I can't answer that question after what happened last night. We should spend more time together and see what happens. I'm not saying no, but right now, things are not at their best with us. I think we need more time to sort things out."

"I understand Cee-Cee, but at least, wear the ring." Tony puts the ring on my finger and says, "Don't ever take this off." Then he kisses my swollen lips.

As the evening goes on, I get up to get dressed and realize that I don't have any clothes. Tony packed all my shit and put it in his Hummer. I wake him up and tell him that I need clothes. It's almost time for me to leave. Tony jets down the stairs and returns with my skinny jeans, a white spaghetti strap top, my Fendi shoes, bag and oversized shades. I pile concealer and foundation on my face in an attempt to hide the marks, but it's not doing a good enough job on the swelling. I am so badly bruised that all I can do is wait for my face to heal. And of course, I have to wear this cheap ass engagement ring. I grab the bag with the money and tell Tony, "I'll call you later."

Tony walks me downstairs to the car and embraces me. Then, I get in the car and leave.

Chapter Seventeen

The Plan

While on my way to Pete's house, I make a quick stop at my sister Sharmaine's place in Queens. I run up in her crib and I tell her to keep this bag for me until next Wednesday. In fact, I tell her that I will be bringing her a bag every day for the next six days.

She says, "No problem sis," and I run out before she can question me about my face.

As I get back into the car, I look in all directions to make sure Tony is not following me. Tony is a nut and I don't trust him as far as I can throw him. So, to ease my mind, I call the apartment and he answers the phone. I am so relieved.

"Hey baby, I just called to see if you were thinking about me," I lie.

"Of course I am. You're my fiancée, making big moves. I love you girl," Tony answers.

"Okay. So, I'll call you later."

"Be good and check in."

I hang up and curse the ground he walks on. I hate this muthafucka and he's gonna pay for what he's done to me. I think, I wanna be there when C-note tears him apart.

When I arrive at Pete's place, I can see he is already standing there waiting for me. He seems to be in a happy mood, so that's a good thing. Pete sees the truck and says, "What's up? I see you didn't give that nigga back his shit." I don't say a word. I just keep my head forward, but when he says C-note called him today, I immediately pull the car over and begin to bawl. Pete reaches over, hugs me and says, "Don't worry. C-note loves you to death." When I look up and Pete sees my face, the look of death is all I see. With gritted teeth and a tight jaw, he asks, "Who did this to you?" I can't answer 'cause too many tears are streaming down my face and there is a lump in my throat.

"It's okay." I finally say. "Some girls tried to jump me last night," I try to lie.

"I don't believe you. Tony beat up on you, didn't he? Didn't he, Cee-Cee?" Pete presses me.

"Pete, please don't make this harder for me. I'll handle it. I got everything under control."

"Nah, fuck that, baby girl. You don't have shit under control. This nigga tried to kill you last night! Why you acting like everything is okay? Well, it isn't. You are C-note's wife and that's my nigga so you know I can't let this shit go down. That nigga is a dead man."

"Please, Pete! Let me handle this. Give me one week. As soon as the last girl makes it through and he gets that off, I'm leaving him. You can find me someone else who can get this weight off like him. Then, he will be cut off completely, so we both got something to do in one week."

"Who the fuck am I gonna get Cee-Cee, when the Bronx Stick Up Chicks are killing and bankrupting all the major players? Once the major players are all gone, the street niggas ain't gonna have no play. So, where do you want me to find this nigga who can do the damn thing?"

"I don't know, but we only got one week. Tony asked me to marry him. I told him that I couldn't make a decision like that after he destroyed my face, but he said to wear the ring anyway. I was too afraid to say no. It's getting serious and dangerous. I know I should never have fucked with him but I did, and believe me, I am regretting it more and more each day. He also wants my connect."

"What? You can't do that Cee-Cee. Brother and Buddy will kill you. What is this nigga up to?"

"I don't know, but he's talking about taking over New York. He says my connect will be the last piece of the puzzle. I don't understand, and I don't want to. I just want to get him out of my life forever."

"Oh my God Cee-Cee, you've created a war. Once we kill Tony, we got to kill his whole family. There's too many brothers and cousins to leave behind and once they get wind of who did it, we become the enemy and they are gonna retaliate. We got one week to find a distributor and put you in hiding. Does he know anything about you and where your people live?"

"No! He doesn't even know about you. I've kept everything a secret. My business is my business. Next week, I'm supposed to tell my connect about him. I think that's why he proposed to me, but I got a trick for his ass. I'm going to be M.I.A., believe me Pete. I'm on point."

"Aiight. One week and one week only. If you don't leave him, I will kill him."

"Okay, can you please drive? I'm in a lot of pain. I just want to relax."

"Yeah girl. Just take it easy."

Chapter Eighteen

Cee-cee's Surprise

The second girl's flight is on time. She made it through smoothly so Pete handles his business quickly and bounces. Luckily, I don't have to wait as long as I did last night. I guess it's because Pete felt sorry for me.

While waiting for Pete in the car, I call Tony. I've been calling Tony every hour on the hour and he's loving it. I tell him that I'll be home by ten o'clock, and he says, "I'm leaving to handle some business, so I'll catch up with you later."

I'm happy about that because I need some time for myself to think about my plan. I am definitely going back to the Hamptons. Nobody knows about that place and I will feel more relaxed there. Pete is going to have to handle everything and I will meet him in Hempstead to finance him ever so often. This is the best way and the only way. I don't think Tony would really go out of his way to find me, but I am not gonna sleep on his ass either.

Finally, back at the apartment, I'm at ease. I walk in and it's quiet, and empty. I put the package up and take my clothes off. I run the water for a bath, get in and soak my body in Calgon. I reach over to the vanity, take out a pack of cigarettes and a blunt. I smoke and chill here for, at least an hour or so.

When I get out of the tub, I slip on my robe and begin to feel queasy. I lay in the bed to rest my head and stomach. My eyes close without hesitation and shortly after my cell rings. I answer, "Hello."

"Hey Tasty, it's me. I'm on my way home and I wanted to know if you want something to eat?"

"Tony, it's 2:30 in the morning. All I want is sleep. No, I'm not hungry."

"Tasty, you didn't eat all day yesterday and you need to feed my baby. I'm a stop at KFC. Get up and roll us a blunt and I'll be there to love you in twenty minutes."

"Aiight Tony. Anything for you."

I put the phone down, turn on the TV and flip through some channels with the remote. I stop at the news on Channel 4. There's a special report. Three niggas from here were murdered over drugs.

"I wonder what street that is?" I say.

While watching the news, I see that the bodies of this guy named Sammy and his two brothers Wayne and Craig, laid out on the ground, riddled with bullet holes.

"Oh my God! What the fuck is going on?"

This must have happened an hour ago. I know these niggas and I can't believe these cats are dead. They are larger than large and push crazy heroin. Tomorrow, I'll call around and find out what happened. It's really time for me to disappear.

I snap out of my trance when I hear the key in the door. I sit up on the bed, open my nightstand drawer and take out the weed to roll the blunt. Tony comes in and asks for the package. He says, "Baby, I gotta make a quick run. I'll be back in a half give me the packages."

I give him another six kilos and he jets out the door. I go to the bathroom, brush my teeth and put some more A&D ointment on my face. I go back to bed and continue to watch the special report. Tears flood my eyes. I can't believe what I am hearing and seeing. One of the reporters is interviewing an eyewitness.

"Why do these people talk to the reporters?" I ask myself.

This young lady, who's in her mid-twenties, is explaining what she saw. She says, "Five females got out of a black Range Rover, walked swiftly to the spot, sprayed it up and ran out with three army bags. I don't know what was in the bags, but they carried them to the truck, threw them in the back and drove off at top speed. These girls have been killing and robbing all the drug dealers. It's crazy out here."

Hearing this shit made me vomit. I jump out of the bed, run to the bathroom and put my head in the toilet bowl. This is too much. Bad things are happening to people I know. I rinse my mouth out in the sink and crawl my ass back to bed. I light the blunt and heard Tony key's in the door again. He comes in, puts the bag of money in the closet and sits next to me. Tony takes the blunt and passes me the food. The smell of it makes my belly begin to rumble. I look in the bag, take the food out and bust down the baked chicken, mashed potatoes, macaroni n' cheese and corn. The Pepsi is kind of flat, but I devour that too. After eating, I take the blunt and smoke until I feel nice. Tony calls out to me and says, "Cee-Cee, look on the dressing table and pass me the bag." I get up and see a bag from Duane Reade. I open it and see that is an advanced EPT.

"What's this Tony?"

"You know what it is."

"Yeah, but it's only been a week. It's too early for anything."

"Nah, I was reading the box, and this advanced one can detect if you're pregnant within two days of sexual intercourse. I want you to have my child so bad that I can't wait to find out if your period is gonna come or not. I wanna be there to see the stick turn pink."

"Tony, this is nonsense. You are setting yourself up for a disappointment."

"Yeah...well, if I'm disappointed, then I know we need to sex more often, and you need to lay up and let my sperm do its job."

"Aiight then! I gotta pee now, so let's see what happens."

Tony and I stroll our asses to the bathroom. I'm praying all the way there that the stick turns blue. I will laugh so hard...silently, of course...and leave his tall ass next week. Tony opens the package and hands it to me. I squat over the bowl and pee on the stick. We have to wait five minutes before the results can be seen so I go back to the bed and continue smoking. Tony follows me.

While relaxing on the bed, smoking my head off, this seems to be the longest five minutes. I turn to Tony and ask, "Did you hear what happened to Sammy and his brothers?"

"Yeah. I drove by and saw a little of it, but I couldn't stick around. I had moves to make."

"I know, but Tony, that's a sad situation. Don't you feel any sympathy? These are people that we know and now they are dead. I'm hurt by it."

"Well, I'm not gonna lose sleep over it. My main concern is, if you're gonna hold a nigga seed down? That's all I wanna know."

Tony gets up, goes to the bathroom and comes out with the coldest eyes ever. He's staring at me real hard. I am scared. I told him that I wouldn't be pregnant and that it might be too early to tell. Tony comes over to the bed, kneels in front of me and open my legs. I'm so terrified that I can't speak. I just hope I don't get another blow to my head. Tony opens my legs wider, exposing my pussy and plants gentle kisses all over my vagina. He kisses and licks with such passion that my pussy creams. He comes up, rubs my stomach, kisses it and then comes face-to-face with me. Tony sticks his tongue in my mouth and looks at me again.

"What's wrong Tony?" I ask.

"Cee-Cee, I love you. In the next month, you need to consider being my wife. I can't have it any other way, especially since you are carrying my baby."

"OH MY GOD TONY! What are you saying?"

Tony reaches into his back pocket and shows the stick to me. It is pink! I want to pass the fuck out. This is not fucking happening to me! No fucking way!

"Tony!"

"Shhh…this is the perfect morning. I want you to make love to me. I want our baby, my son, to feel the love from the both of us."

Tony rolls onto his back and rolls me on top of him. He brings my head down to his mouth and kisses me hard. I try to ease out of his crushing embrace but he holds me tight. One hand is on the back of my head and the other hand is palming my ass. He gyrates upwards through his jeans, rubbing his hardness on my bare front. Slowly, my body responds and even though I can't believe what is happening to me, I'm getting turned on. There is no doubt in my mind that I'm leaving him, and this baby won't stop me. But, for right now, I'll let him enjoy me. It's best to play it his way until I get what I want. Instantly, my mood changes and instead of him forcing me, I'm all over him. I aggressively work my tongue into his mouth and then on his neck. I help him come up out of his shirt and jeans. I take off his boxers and put his dick in my hand. I jerk his dick tightly. This makes him moan loudly. Then, I kiss it. I kiss and lick all over it. When I get his dick real nice and hard, I plant my entire mouth over it and swallow his balls.

"God damn Cee-Cee! How do you do that?" he asks through clenched teeth.

I come up slowly on it and suck his head until it glistens. Tony cries out in pleasure. I put my mouth back on it again and deep throat. I bob my head up and down, faster and faster like a woodpecker pecking wood and then stop. While he's trying to catch his breath, I climb on top and squat over his dick and insert it inside of me. I bounce my fat ass on him like a jockey on a stallion. I ride, stretch his cock outward, inward, circle it and grind it. I'm out of control and full of energy. Tony grips my hips and guides me as he fucks me from below. I cry out in ecstasy, calling his name, cummin' hard while slowing down my tempo. Tony turns me over on my back and pumps some serious blows to my belly. My legs are wrapped around his back and he is not playing. I pinch Tony's nipples and suck on them. Tony's body jerks and as his balls clap against my ass, he screams, "I love you. I'm gonna marry you. This is my pussy and I can't wait for you to have my baby," and then cums hard, wild and long.

For what seems like hours, we lay in each other arms and cuddle as I'm listening to Tony's plans for the future, about all these wonderful things that will never happen…like me and the baby. In the midst of all his talking, he sits up and says, "I got a surprise for you. Let's take a shower, get dressed and go somewhere." I agree and we did just that.

Driving out to Kew Gardens in Queens, we pull up in front of this gray and white house. This shit is nice for the average. We get out and walk up to the door. I was expecting Tony to ring the doorbell, but instead, he reaches in his pocket, takes out a key and puts it in the lock. When he opens the door he says, "Welcome home Tasty! This is our brand-new house."

I am shocked and disgusted but with a fake-ass smile, I show my appreciation. I hug him and jump up and down like a schoolgirl. Tony takes me by the hand shows me around the house. It's a single-family house with three bedrooms and two baths. It also, has a porch, fireplace, basement and attic. Tony takes me into the garage and there is a brand new, fully loaded silver Yukon, sitting on thirty-two-inch rims. I jump on him again, but this time I go all out with the bullshit "I love you's." Tony gives me the keys to the SUV and I crank up the engine, telling him, "Let's go for a ride."

We go shopping for more clothes, furniture and decorations for the house. It has truly been, an exhausting day and I am in need of some rest. I watch Tony do the unpacking and the excitement that is written all over his face shows that he feels like a king. I don't give a fuck though, 'cause I am leaving his black ass with his dick in his hand. I belong to C-note and he is my real and only true love…my soul mate.

Chapter Nineteen

Creating New Business

The last week has been really stressful, especially since I've spent most of it moving into this new house with Tony; not to mention the anxiety of being pregnant. C-note doesn't know what is going on yet but as soon as I leave Tony, he will. Tony has been doing everything right. As soon as I get the work, he knocks them off and comes straight home. He got me on some wifey shit. I'm just gonna play the part until it's time to say farewell. Tony fucked up. All he had to do was play the part of being my lover. All this beating up on me and disrespecting C-note is a no-no. I fucked up too but I can distinguish the difference between a fuck and wanting to be someone's lover. There's no way I can get carried away by good dick. It takes more than that. Yeah, it might do the job for the moment but a reality check will always bring me home. My heart is for C-note. He is all I want. The only way we could ever end our relationship is through death, so we're happily stuck with each other for life.

Tonight, I'm supposed to be meeting up with Pete. We are going to discuss our new plan and I'm going to meet this new guy he got. Since tomorrow is my last day with Tony, I need to get everything in order. I want this done nice n' smooth. Tony also thinks I'm going to introduce him to my connect. I told him that I am having a meeting with them tonight and I will set a day for them to meet. He is really excited about that because he said, "This will be the last piece of the puzzle." But little does he knows, he is going to get fucked. I wish I could see the expression on his face tomorrow night when he realizes that I am gone for good. In fact, I'm going to write him a letter telling him how I feel. He's gonna be one mad mother but fuck him. Does he honestly believe I can love him and stay with him after he beat the shit out of me and knocked me out? Nah! He got me fucked up. I hate his ass. I'm going to fuck him real good tonight, then leave him. I might as well do me in the process. The one thing I'm glad for is that he doesn't know my family. He doesn't know shit about me. The only person he knows is Stacy and she doesn't know shit herself so, where is he gonna look? I can see it now. No Tasty, no baby and no connect.

It's almost time for me to meet up with Pete so I call my sister and tell her, "I'll be over there by ten pm tomorrow to pick up the bags, so be home." So, that is set. I put on some casual shit and head out the door to Pete's place. Everything is falling into place and I feel worry-free. Tomorrow night can't come fast enough but I've got to be patient.

I pull up in front of Pete's place and spot a fully-loaded, black Honda Accord. The way this baby is blasting his sounds makes me think there is a block party in the area. I park and dial Pete's cell to let him know I'm here. Pete picks up and tell me to go to the Red Lobster on Queens Blvd and reserve a table for four. I am pissed but in a nice tone, I agree. I pull off again and I'm on my way there. I hate going to Red Lobster. Everybody and their mother goes there and the service is really bad. But hey, if that's where they want to eat, then so be it. Just as long as we get the business in full swing. A lot of shit is about to go down and I'm ready.

As I pull up in front of another ghetto ass restaurant, I find a parking space and put two dollars in the meter. I stroll three stores down, enter Red Lobster and get a table for four. I sit down, order a virgin strawberry daiquiri with no liquor and chill. I look around the room and see that it's quite packed. There is a group of men at a table and they are eyeing me down. They keep talking to one another and staring at me. I don't pay them any mind because I get this reaction all the time. One of the guys who is tall and slim with a bald head, whispers something to the waitress. She walks out of sight and five minutes later, she comes to my table with a bottle of Moet. She points at the table of men and says, "This is from Danny, the tall bald guy."

I smile and say, "Tell Danny that I said, thanks but no thanks. I'm not drinking tonight, so in return, I will put this on my card, and they can enjoy it." She walks back over to the men's table with the bottle and relays the message. Danny holds up the bottle with a smile and wink, letting me know he welcomes my Mo.

After sitting there for ten minutes, I grow frustrated. I look at my watch and say, "What the fuck is the problem?" I take my cell out of my bag, turn it on and dial Pete.

Pete answers and says, "What's up?"

"Aren't you and your new friends supposed to be here? You got me sitting in this place looking stupid with a fucking table for four."

"Girl, they are right there watching you and so far they are impressed," Pete tells me.

"What do you mean…they're watching me?"

"Yeah, I guess you can get up now from your table and go have dinner with the guys and your returned Moet."

"What? So, y'all playing me?"

"Just go handle your business. I already did my part."

We hang up, I put the tip on the table and get up like I'm about to leave. I walk towards the door and dip into the lady's room. After freshening up, I walk back into the main dining area, walk over to their table and say, "Gentlemen, I do believe this seat is for me."

They all look up. Danny stands up and pulls out my chair. I sit, order another round of drinks for them and water for me. The waitress comes back and we order our meals. The table is filled with a lot of raw and baked oysters, lobsters, king and snow crab legs and all different types of shrimp. This is definitely a feast. We eat, talk, bullshit, laugh and when the table got cleared, we get down to business.

My opening speech is, "Don't play me because I am a woman. Don't try to fuck me because I have a cunt and don't try to rob me because I'm gangsta. I will, without hesitation, order a hit. There's a lot of power behind me and I wish not to use it. Everything can go smooth for a very long time and we can be a family with mad love. If I'm coming off too aggressive and if you don't like my tone, then that's not my problem. That's yours. We can always get up from this table and part ways without any misunderstandings but, if you decide to deal with me, then I'm a give it to you raw."

All four guys look at me and then at each other. Danny, of course clears his throat and says, "I respect your gangsta, but threats are not necessary. Doing business is not a problem. In fact, I've been waiting for someone like you because you can provide a lot of weight. I got the spots and I got people all over who want good, pure shit. I'm not here to hurt you. I'm not here to fuck you. I'm not here to take advantage of you. I love the fact that I'm dealing with a woman. Now, I can't front, even though you are very attractive, but business is business. I'm the head nigga in charge and these are my people. Pete already met these niggas, so when I'm not around, you can deal with them also."

"No baby, you deal with Pete. You will never see my face again. Whatever you and your people need, just let Pete know and I'll make it happen. Just stay alive and keep your dick in your pants."

"I know that's right. I heard about them girls. They are ruthless but, we got everything under control."

"Okay, so how much are you looking to purchase at a time?"

"Starting next month, I need two to three hundred keys at fifteen gees a pop. I hope that's not putting a strain on you. If that's too much for you to handle, then speak now and we can work something out. Also, coming up in the near future, I'm thinking about working with some heroin. I'm willing to pay eighty gees for the real Mccoy."

"I hear that. I can handle the shipment and I'll work on the heroin but let me ask you this. Are you that large to pay all the money when the shipment comes?"

"No."

"NO! So why am I sitting here wasting my fucking time?"

"Because I am a man that needs your help. You got your shit together, and I know who you are. I've been to your house in the Hamptons and I've done business with Brother and C-note. I got crazy shit on lock where I'm from, but I don't have enough product to keep the business alive. You're large, and you can make a lot of things happen and this will also prove to you, Brother and C-note that I'm worthy. If I was gaming you, I wouldn't have said shit. I could have let Pete bring the shipment, killed him and built from that but that's not my style. All I got is my word and trust. So, go hold a meeting with Brother and C-note, tell them Blue-Eye Danny is back on the scene and needs help. I just need the first two shipments to be on consignment and from then on, everything else will be paid in full. I know you're running the business, so let's take it all the way. Don't shut me down. Just give me a chance."

"This shipment is a lot to be just taking a chance but I respect your honesty. For that, I don't have to talk to Brother or C-note. I am the decision-maker for now. I'll let them know what I'm doing. So, you got two weeks to get your spot and people in order because when the work comes, it will be on a constant flow. I'm willing to take a chance with you so, you got a deal. How long do you think it will take you to knock off that shipment?'

"One month or less."

"Okay, I want all the money, all cash one month from delivery and you will deal with Pete only. If anyone else comes around, they are not my people."

"Thanks for this! I won't let you down," Danny says gratefully.

We talk some more and then part ways. I get in my truck and head home with a smile on my face thinking about the meeting. I can't believe that I'm gonna push that much weight and I can't believe I agreed for the first two shipments to be on consignment. Buddy is going to spaz the fuck out but something tells me this is gonna be better than wonderful. All I need him to do is release some of the shipments that come through the port for me and it's a wrap. I will make up for this mishap with Tony.

Speaking of Tony...tonight is going to be a night he won't never forget. It's eight o'clock and I'm going home to get everything ready for my wonderful evening. I already got the bottle of Dom chilling in the fridge. I'm a roll three fat-ass blunts, take out my white teddy, garter belt, and shear mid-thigh robe. I'm also going to lay out his white silk boxers and pajama top set. I already ate so I'm full. I'm just waiting for the evening to begin.

As I approach my house, I notice Tony's Hummer is here. I pull into the driveway and park. I get out, step into my home and see that Tony is chilling in the living room waiting for me. He looks so good. I walk up to him and give him the biggest hug ever. He puts his arms around my waist, I sit on his lap and we kiss. I pull away from him and say, "Lets take a shower and get cozy for the rest of the evening."

We walk upstairs, I turn on the shower and go meet him in the bedroom. We take our clothes off and enter the shower together. As we bathe one another, it doesn't take long for us to get turned on. Tony asks me, "What do you want?" and I answer, "For you to get on your knees and eat me." Tony obliges with the quickness, and I put one leg up on the edge of the tub. The water is beating down on us, and the temperature is just right. This feels so good. Tony parts my pussy lips, pulls my hood back to expose my clit and sucks my little bud. Immediately, my legs begin to tremble because he is attacking my weak spot head-on. I'm grabbing the back of his head and moaning with pleasure. I tell him, "While you're eating my pussy, I want you to jerk your dick." Tony positions his tongue on my click, sticks his thumb inside of me and grabs his python. Damn, this looks good and feels even better. We are going to take it to the extreme and knock each other out with sex. After tonight, the next time I get some dick will be when C-note gets his furlough or when he gets out, but I can wait.

Fucking around with niggas is dangerous. While I stand here grinding on his face, he aggressively finger fucks me. I feel my first shock of waves erupting. I grab onto his head and move it up and down like I am washing clothes on a wash board. He is driving me wild.

"Tony, I'm cummin' baby."

"Cum Tasty. Put it all in my mouth and let me stick this big dick up in your guts."

I'm moaning, calling out his name and cummin'. Tony slurps up all my sweetness, comes up off his knees and turns me around. I'm slightly bent over as he sticks his huge hunk of manhood inside of me. This shit got us in a frenzy and we are wildin' out. Tony is in love with me. I can feel it. It's a shame I got to do him dirty but that's what has to happen.

"I love you, Tony and I'm glad I'm having you baby," I moan.

Tony pulls his dick out, turns me around to face him, lifts me up, puts his dick back inside, sticks his tongue in my mouth and continues making love to me. The way he lifts me up and rams his dick inside of me makes me feel like a doll. He has full control without any struggle, and I bounce on him real hard.

"Cee-Cee I love you girl. Don't ever leave me."

As he grunts, moans and thrusts, Tony cums inside of me. He grinds my body on his, so all of his cum enters upwards.

"I love you. I love you, Cee-Cee," Tony moans.

"I love you too, Tony," I lie.

Tony keeps me pinned up against the shower wall for a minute and loves me hard. After we simmer down and catch our breaths, we continue to wash up and we get out. We walk back over to our room and put on the sleepwear that I had laid out for us. I run down the stairs, get the bottle of Dom Perignon and two champagne glasses and bring them back upstairs.

Tony asks, "What's the occasion?"

I tell him, "Tonight, we are going to celebrate a lot of things. First, this is the last time I will be smoking and drinking because of the baby. I want a strong and healthy son, so I'm a take it to the extreme and get fucked up one last time. Second, my peoples are willing to meet you. I told them that you had a lot to offer and that you can move weight, so you will be meeting them the day after tomorrow. And third, I've decided to become your wife and we can do it anytime this month. I love you and I'm sorry if I ever made you mad at me. Please forgive me. From this day on, I will be the perfect girl.

I love you Tony."

"I love you too and having you in my life is all I want and need."

We lay in each other's arms, talk and watch three movies. We are so high and drunk that the last lovemaking turns into a drunken, simple fuck.

Chapter Twenty

Leaving Tony

Waking up with Tony in my arms feels so good. I love the comfort of a man being next to me because I am a passionate woman. If Tony was a different person, then I wouldn't mind waking up with him and sharing his bed every night, but things happen for a reason and his abuse wasn't meant to be. I don't mind going through the pregnancy on my own. C-note is my future husband and he is the father of my child. C-note already decided that, if I am pregnant, he wants me to keep the baby. That is a manly decision. I love him and I can't wait to speak to him in the comfort of our own home.

Watching Tony sleep peacefully, I shake my head. I feel sorry about the decision I've made, but a girl got to do what a girl got to do. I reach for Tony's face and caress it. He is so gorgeous. While he lay there sound asleep, I move my hand all over his body. God, he is tight and cut. I love it. I reach for his soft and heavy manhood, stare at it and lick my dry lips. I love his dick. It fills me up completely and the harder it gets, the more it weighs. I move my head down to lay on his stomach, stare at it some more and decide to suck it slowly. I put Tony's semi-hard dick in my mouth and wiggle my tongue around it. He sighs and caresses my shoulders. While I tease his dick in and out of my mouth, I feel him growing harder and harder. I get up on my elbow with his dick down my throat, come up to the tip of the head and kiss it. I kiss, tongue, nibble and suck the head only as I jerk his shaft. Tony tightens up his body, breathing out of control. I pull the skin of his dick back as far as it will go, hold it there and bob my tightly cuffed lips on it. That brings Tony's moans to a soprano. Tony grabs my head and upwardly fucks my mouth. I loosen up my hand grip and deep throat on it. Tony knows my mouth is powerful. I am the *toe-curler and the eye in the back of your head roller.* Yes, I am fierce. I take my fingertips and play with his balls. He opens up his legs and screams out, "Suck your dick mommy."

I come up off the dick, jerk it softly and say, "You want me to suck it daddy? Huh?'

"Yes, mommy suck it. I want you to suck it until I cum."

"After I suck it and you cum down my throat, what are you going to give me? Are you going to show me who daddy is? Are you going to put something on me that I'll never forget?"

"Yes! Yes! Suck it, mommy, 'cause when I get this first nut off, don't tell me to stop. I'm going to terrorize your pussy, and I got a trick for that ass. I love you baby, and you belong to me. I own you."

I put my hot, watering mouth back on his dick and give him what he asks for. Tony is sick and can't understand how I do it. I got him mouth and pussy-whipped. I go down on that ten-inch with ease. I suck his dick with expertise. Tony arches his back up off the bed. His head is on the pillow and his legs are cocked open and I'm between them sucking sparks out of him. Tony is mentally gone. He looks like a bitch with no sense right now and l love it. As he fucks my throat hard and his dick swells, Tony squirts some cum out and calls my name like a madman. Then, he lets out globs of hot, thick cum. Tony moans and groans like if he's in pain and I continuously bob my head on it as I drink every last drop. When I finish sucking him off, I climb on top of him, put his semi-hard dick inside of me and ride his cock back to life. I grind on it real slow. I love to slow fuck. Slow fucking makes me cum real quick and keep my pussy wet and warm. Tony reaches up and grabs my titties. He sucks on them, making my nipples fully erect. I lean my head back and arch my back so he can get a better suck and feel. I bounce my fat ass on his pole. I'm loving it and I want to cum. Tony upwards fucks my pussy and as he comes up, I bounce hard on it. As my body shakes, I cry out in ecstasy, calling out his name and cum all down his dick. Tony holds me tight so he can feel the juices of my cream.

The morning is turning out to be overwhelming. I haven't even smoked any weed and I feel high. I roll off Tony and lay on my back, trying to catch my breath. Tony rolls halfway on top of me and massages my stomach so passionately that I can feel his love. Tears well up in my eyes because I realize I do have feelings for him. Yes,

I'm in love with C-note, but Tony got a little hold on me too.

"Tony, I love you," I whisper.

He looks up and sees my tears. He comes face-to-face with me and whispers, "I love you too Tasty."

Tony kisses me gently and parts my legs as his dick finds its way to my honeycomb. It's so wet and ready that his dick goes in with ease. He is extremely hard and I know that within a couple of minutes, his gentle fucking is gonna work into a wild frenzy. Tony keeps his long tongue in my mouth and picks up the tempo of the motion of his hips. Some long strokes with power came at me and some short strokes to the walls digs in me. I scratch and dig my nails into his back, but it doesn't faze him. When Tony's mind takes him there, he doesn't feel scratches, digs or hear his name being called. Even though sometimes, it can be a bit much, I still love his penetration. Tony puts my legs on his shoulders and locks my arms around his. He relentlessly pumps his hardcore dick inside of me. I scream in pleasure and release my second wave of cum. Tony moans all types of fuck me talk and says, "I'm glad you creamed my dick again because I got something special for you." Tony thrusts himself inside of me and then pulls his dick out. He leans up off me a little bit but keeps my arms locked and my legs in the air. Tony reaches for his dick, looks at me say, "Just relax." Before I can say a word, I feel his hard-ass dick pressing against my asshole, trying to enter my forbidden spot.

"Tony no!" I yell, but he forces his tongue into my mouth to keep me from yelling. I cry in agony as I feel my flesh being stretched and I feel so weak. I bite Tony's tongue and bottom lip, but he keeps on pushing through. Hysterically, I bawl. I am so mad because I am being violated in the worst way. This is definitely rape. Tony finally takes his tongue out of my mouth, and he's bleeding while his dick lays five inches deep inside of me. I scream and beg Tony to take it out. I let him know how much it hurts, but he just buries his head in my neck.

He keeps his dick still and says, "Don't move. It's gonna be alright. Get used to it because this is now a part of our lives. It's gonna hurt the first couple of time, but after that, you will grow to love it. Tasty, you're probably gonna want me to fuck you more in your ass than your hot, sweet pussy."

"No Tony! Please get up. This is wrong, disgusting, painful and a complete violation. I don't want this. If you love me and have respect for me, then you will honor my wishes."

Tony doesn't say another word. He slowly pulls his dick out. My head is so light and the excruciating pain is making my body so weak. I have never felt so disrespected. I would have preferred the beatings.

Tony slowly works his dick inside of me again, ignoring my screams. He stays at the same five inches and fucks my ass. Tony keeps me pinned up and hurt for twenty minutes until he finally cums. As Tony busts his nut, he screams loud in my ears and rams the whole ten inches inside of me with hard jerks. By this time, I am like a zombie with a dick up my ass. Tony drains his dick and lets it soften it way out of me. When he finally rolls off, I slowly unpin my cramped body, ball up and cry. I cry so loud and say to myself, "I am leaving your ass tonight."

Tony grabs me from behind and cradles me. I allow him to do this only because I got something more painful for his ass.

Hours later, he goes to the bathroom, takes a shower, cleans the tub and runs a warm bath for me. After he helps me get in, he goes downstairs to the kitchen to make some breakfast. I'm truly disgusted and full of tears. I can't wait to leave. While taking my time in the tub, Tony comes back upstairs with a tray of food. He walks into the bathroom, so I get out of the tub and sit on the bed with just a towel wrapped around me. He brings the tray to me and we both eat. While I'm eating, I ask, "Why did you do that to me?" and his response is, "Because we need to spice thing up and try different things."

"Fuck you nigga," I said in my head, smile and say, "Give me some time to get used to it, boo."

We engage in some small talk for a little while until Tony tells me he has to make a run at five, so he'll be home late.

That is perfect because my plan can now fall into place without a problem. Earlier, I was feeling a little guilty about walking out on him, but after he violated my body, I'm back to my original thinking...FUCK HIM!

"Tony, since you're gonna be gone, I'm going to hang out with Stacy for a while. I think it's time for me to tell her that I'm pregnant and if you don't mind, I would like for her to be our baby's godmother."

"Oh yeah? Sure. I didn't think about it, but yeah that's cool. Also, while you're there, y'all should also start making our wedding arrangements."

"Well, how much are you willing to spend on this wedding?"

"You can take it to the extreme. I love you, so it doesn't matter. Just make sure it's beautiful."

I move the tray from in front of me. I get my painful ass up and walk over to closet to get me some clothes to wear. I put make-up on my face and wrap my hair into a ponytail. As I'm getting myself together, I look over my shoulder and Tony is getting ready too. I can't even front, he is a fine ass murthfucka. As we finish getting dressed, Tony decides we should leave now so we can get back home early. I walk him to the door, hug him and kiss him everlastingly. It is so intense and passionate that we both got turned on. I pull away, back up and look at his hard ass dick calling my name. I hug him again and grind on it, telling him how much I love him, and I can't wait to give him my surprise tonight. Tony opens the door and hauls ass into his Hummer.

I run up the stairs like a madwoman, all sore and shit. I get my jewelry box, open it up and decide I don't need these. I'm a leave everything so he can be reminded of me. I open my drawer and take out a notepad and pen. I write a nice goodbye letter and put it on my pillow with the engagement ring. I jump in the Yukon and speed over to my sister, Sharmaine's place. I call her and tell her that I'm not too far away, so get the bags together, I'm in a hurry. When I pull up at her house, she is already there, standing on her porch with six large duffle bags. I jump out and tell her that I love her and to put the bags in the truck. I get back in my truck and drive to Stacy's house. I don't let her know that I'm coming because I'm not doing the chit chat shit today. So, I'll park the truck in front of her house, put the keys in the glove compartment and hail a cab and be on my way.

Chapter Twenty-One

Tony's Nightmare

While driving back home, I'm a bit upset because Cee-Cee didn't call me all day. I guess the girls talk must have had a hell of a talk. Of course, it would be because I'm a hell of a guy but, regardless of how good and interesting the girl talk was, she still should have kept her phone on so I can hear her sweet voice. I just love me some Cee-Cee. Her having my baby and being my wife-to-be is more than any man can ask for. One thing for sure, they will never want for nothing. Tomorrow, I will meet these people she works with and then I will be the man. Shit will definitely be my way or no way. Niggas will hate, but that's all a part of the game.

As I reminisce on our earlier events, I can't believe I had anal sex with Cee-Cee. That shit felt so fucking good that my balls are tingling right now. Damn! She drives me wild. I ain't never had a woman make me feel as good or as tight as she does. Cee-Cee's head game is off the hook. I've had plenty of girls suck my dick but none of them had me standing on my tippy toes or cocking my legs up while they deep throat my dick. Yeah! She screams a lot, but that's only because her pussy is so tight. I zone out and lose control. WOW! My dick is rock hard. I can't wait to get home. I'm gonna tear that ass up. Speaking of ass. That was some insane shit. I know I hurt her but I could not help myself. I've fucked plenty of girls in their asses but that was with a condom and they shit was stretched out. Bitches these days, whether they are young or old, they shit be worn out. They fuck so many niggas that you can't even bust a good nut. Cee-Cee's pussy is the kind that would make you kill a muthafucka. It snaps back. I know C-note didn't even beat that pussy up. He kept that pussy tight and right for me and I will make love to it all day and night for the rest of my life. Now that she is up for our new anal sex activity, whenever she is on her period or on her six weeks recovery from childbirth, I can still have fun. I don't mind jerking my dick sometimes, but not all the time. I'll just K-Y jelly that fat ass and pleasure the both of us. I don't know why I am tormenting myself right now. My dick is aching for her.

I pull up on the block and I don't see Cee-Cee's truck in the driveway. Maybe she's parked in the garage. I electronically open the gate, pull in and walk to my door. When I open it up, all the lights are off but it would be. It's two o'clock in the morning. I walk straight to the kitchen and take a Heineken out of the fridge. I walk to the living room, sit for a moment and spark the blunt that was left in the ashtray. I'm smoking and drinking, getting real nice to go upstairs to make sweet love to my future wife. I strip out of my clothes and get naked. While sitting here, feeling my buzz and watching my dick rise, I jerk it. My dick is fully erect, so I walk up the stairs, enter the dark room and reach for Cee-Cee. I feel for her, but all I feel is an empty bed. I turn the night light on and a rage of fire flares out of my nostrils.

"I'M A KILL THIS BITCH!" I yell.

No fucking wife of mine is gonna be out of my house past two o'clock in the morning. My dick instantly goes limp. I sit at the foot of the bed, look up at her pillow and see something blinging and an envelope. I move closer to the pillow, grab the envelope and realize that what's blinging is Cee-Cee's engagement ring. My heart is pounding as I open the envelope and read:

Dear Tony,

I know you are in a fucked-up state of mind because I am not there and not wearing your ring, but this is all your fault. I tried to spare you this heartbreak and I even had second thoughts about leaving you, but this morning was the last fucking straw. You beat me up twice, stopped my relationship with C-note and violated me in the worst way. I can no longer forgive you. I'm so disgusted that I don't want you in my life. You don't have anything to offer but a good fuck. Financially, I don't need you. My shit is where it's at. You getting me pregnant is a mishap, but I'm happy and I will raise our baby to the best of my ability. I want you to find someone else and try to be happy. Just don't come looking for me. You will never find me. Your Yukon is parked in front of Stacy's house. I left my key in the glove compartment. Stacy doesn't know what's going on, but if you wish to make an ass out of yourself by telling her, then be my guest. I love you, but I got to go. Take care!

Tasty

I scream, "BITCH! BITCH! BITCH!" at the top of my lungs with tears in my eyes. I pick up the cell and call Cee-Cee a hundred times, hoping she'll answer so I can apologize but she don't. I'm hurt! My heart is fucked up and I need both of them…her and my baby. How could she just walk out and leave me? I go to the closet and look in the drawer and nothing is gone. She didn't take anything. Maybe she's just blowing off steam, trying to teach me a lesson. I'll give her that. I've been a complete asshole and when she comes home, I promise to make it right. Tomorrow, I'll pick up the truck and wait for her to come home. I know she'll be back and I'll love her the way she wants to be loved. Tony Jr. is growing and I need to be there every step of the way.

Chapter Twenty-Two

Free At Last

Damn! I wish I could smoke a blunt right now, but those days are over until I have my baby. It feels real good to be at home and to be myself. I will never try to live a life other than what I know again. Moving uptown was a huge mistake, but it's all good. Things worked out for the best and little does Tony know; I am that bitch. I know, right now he is gutted. He can't find me. He doesn't know my real name, where I live, who my family is or anything. I might have fallen and bumped my head on some good dick, but I'm conscious now. I'm not gonna say that I won't think about him from time to time, but he is a thing of the past.

As my mind gets weary and my eyes close, I feel myself falling into a deep sleep.

Startled by the phone, I open my eyes and see that it's a pre-paid call from C-note. I quickly press five and cry, "I love you baby."

"Cee-Cee, you're home?" C-note asks.

"Yes, C-note. I told you I'd get away from him. He's crazy and I planned it right. I love you, and I'm sorry for everything."

"How are you?"

"I'm good…and pregnant."

"What?"

"Yeah, I'm pregnant."

"You think it's my baby?"

"C-note, I pray and hope it is, but no matter what, I want this baby to be yours."

"Well, let us pray for that and no matter what, I love you and that's my child. So, when do you think you'll be able to come see me?"

"I won't. Tony is going to be looking for me and I can't have him find me or know where we live. Tony is crazy enough to stake out you and Brother's jails to see if I show up."

"Okay I understand, so just hold your head up. I already spoke to my case manager about my camp status and everything looks good, so I'm hoping to be at camp next month. Brother too. Did he call you yet?"

"No, but I'm sure he'll call today. I miss you baby."

"I love you for real. Don't worry about anything. Just take care of yourself and my baby."

"I will and call me as much as you can."

"Give me a kiss and go back to sleep."

After giving him a kiss over the phone, I hang up and hug my pillow. I thank God for bringing me out of that dangerous environment and for keeping C-note in my life. I love him and I'll never hurt him again. While deep in thought, I'm interrupted by my vibrating cell phone. I get up to look at it, and it's Tony. Immediately, my heart pounds and I become nervous. Why, I don't know? He can't touch me so, I should answer the phone, right? But I don't. He is a thing of the past and I got to move on. I let the cell ring out and notice I have twenty-five messages. Twenty-four of them of from him and I reluctantly listen to the messages. Some are verbally abusive, and some are pleads. I erase them all and return Stacy's call because hers sounds urgent. I hope she's alright. After a couple of rings, she answers, "It's about fucking time bitch!"

"Yeah, I know. What's the deal?"

"You! I'm a fuck you up. How the fuck are you pregnant and didn't tell me shit?"

"Who told you that? How do you know that?" I ask, although I already know the answer.

"How do you think? You drove your truck over here and parked it in front of my house. Then, Tony bangs down my door like a madman, demanding for you to come out of my house. He wakes up the neighbors, walks in my place and searches my shit looking for you. My man Spin is in the bed and Tony put his Glock in his mouth, trying to make me tell him where you're at. He wouldn't believe me when I said that I didn't know. I'm screaming and crying, going out of my mind, trying to convince him that I don't know shit. Then, he tells me that you left him and that you're pregnant with his baby. He said that if you don't come home, he's gonna find you and kill you. This nigga is not playing, so you should either just go home or call him. I don't want his crazy ass fucking my shit up with my men. It's bad enough that I'm cheating on Clive by fucking Spin."

"Oh my God! I'm so sorry that happened. I knew he would freak out, but I didn't think he would react like that. Yes, I am pregnant, but I can't be with Tony. He's dangerous. He's a woman-beater. He already beat me up twice because of C-note and C-note is my future husband. It's bad enough that I got pregnant, but this nigga is taking shit to the extreme. He wants marriage and the whole nine yards, and I can't give him that. I'm sorry you're involved, but I'm not coming back around there. I'm not coming to hang out with you. I got to stay away. The only contact we will have is on this cell. Other than that, I can't trust it. C-note is already pissed off, but we are getting our shit back on track."

"I hear that. So, what do you want me to tell him if he comes back around my way looking for you?"

"Tell him you haven't seen me and that you can't reach me by phone."

"Aiight."

"What about Spin? Is he gonna put the heat to Tony's ass?"

"I don't know. That nigga was so pissed off. When he left, he palmed my face with his hand and pushed me on the floor, but that's what I get for being hot in the ass. Spin got a bomb as dick though but fuck him. Instead of mushing me, he should have jumped his bad ass in Tony's face. Niggas always show a sign of pussy when a real nigga is in their ass, but it's cool."

"So, what's been going on?"

"Diamond and Platinum got robbed last night by them broads. Those bitches took everything. Coke, weed, jewelry and bundles of money. They are not playing out here. I'm glad they didn't kill them. Those niggas are alright. They won't be able to live up to their names anymore, but they're still cool with me."

"Damn girl! That's fucked up. All the big willies are falling hard. I hope they get a chance to rise again. Anyway, I'm a go lay down and I'll keep you posted. Don't worry. I won't cut you off. You will hear from me all the time."

"Okay. I love you and be careful."

"One!"

Man, what is really going on out there? Who are these hoes? What are they trying to do? Whatever it is, it better not affect me. I got money to make. I pick up my cell and call Pete to find out what's the deal and how everything going.

"Cee-Cee! What's the deal baby?" he asks.

"You! Did you do what I asked you to do?"

"Yeah. When are you coming out to play?"

"At one."

"Meet me on Springfield and Hempstead."

"Okay, I'll be driving a white Benz S-Class."

"We'll talk when I see you."

"Aiight."

I hang up the phone feeling good and bubbly. After I shower, eat and get dressed. I'm ready to make some moves. I feed Pus-Pus and decide to take her with me. I take a final look around my place and we leave.

Pus-Pus and I cruise down the L.I.E headed in the Queens direction. It takes us about an hour and fifteen minutes, but we are right on time. I parked on the corner and wait for a few minutes and then Pete pulls up behind me. He gets out, sits in my passenger seat and questions me to death.

"This is a bad-ass whip. Who lent it to you?"

"If you looked on the license plate, you would have seen the initials BCB. That represents something."

"I know what it stands for. So, is it over between you and that nigga?"

"Yep! It's a done deal. I left his ass yesterday afternoon and he's going ballistic, but that's his bad, not mine."

"Yeah, I know that's right. Just don't be a fool and go back to him. Leave that madness alone. You already know what he is capable of doing."

"So, what you got for me?"

"So far, I got ten females lined up. I already made their reservations. None of them know each other, so two are leaving at the same time and returning at the same time. I need forty geez to handle everything. Also, Buddy gave me the ok to take one of the shipment containers that's coming off the pier to secure your deal."

"Ok, good. When do you have to pick up the tickets?"

"Tomorrow, before five."

"Okay, so we'll meet…same time, same place tomorrow. I'll bring sixty because I want you to work on getting the next ten girls ready. Have photos and flight times ready for each girl."

"Okay, I'm a do that right now."

"Call me later. If I don't answer my phone, leave a message and I'll get back to you. It's off now because I don't want to talk to Tony."

"Cool, I got you."

Pete exits my car, and I drive off, heading back to the Hamptons. No rush, no obligations and no worries. I'm just chilling.

Chapter Twenty-Three

Booming Business

It's been a month since I left Tony. It was hard in the beginning not having him around, but now, I'm used to it. Tony calls my cell day and night, but I don't return his calls. I've heard that he still lives at the house and that the Yukon is still parked in the driveway. No women have been seen coming out of that place, so I guess he's too busy trying to find me to play the field. It's all good and I wish him all the best. I'm six weeks into my pregnancy. Not showing yet, but the morning sickness has kicked in. My clothes are getting a bit tight and I've noticed that my breasts are firmer. I'm ecstatic. C-note calls me every day for updates on my pregnancy. I can't wait for him to come home. Being pregnant makes me extra horny. The sooner he gets to camp, the sooner I can feel him again. I need my C-note. I want my C-note. I love my C-note.

Well, the last two weeks have been really good. Danny got the shipment he wanted and paid me in full yesterday. I was quite pleased with the outcome. I knew he would come through. Two hundred and fifty keys is a lot to give someone on consignment but as my Pop would say, "You got to trust somebody sometimes," and I'm glad I did. He received 250 keys and I made $3,750,000. Tell me I ain't that bitch. Shit! This is more than doing the most. If I can make this amount every month, I'll have close to fifty mill by the time Brother and C-note get home. I just hope everything continues to run smoothly because this is business. Big business. Buddy is coming to New York for a week next month, and I can't wait to show him my new vault. I think the reason he is coming is because he doesn't believe that I got rid of all that work and got paid so well that I could request more keys out of the containers. Yeah, shit is like that and he'll see for himself. I ain't trying to conquer NY, but NY is able to eat because of me. Shit was really scarce out there. The streets are crying and the niggas are dying. I'm glad I'm not out there like that. How I run my business is official and Fed free. I just feel extra powerful like that.

Chapter Twenty-Four

Tony Got Game

I can't believe this bitch left me. She disappeared without a trace and nobody knows where she's at. It's bad enough that I don't know her family and I could kick myself in the ass for that. How could I have been so stupid? That should have been one of the first things I did, but it's all good because I do believe I'm going to find her. This time, I'll make it right. I won't hit her. She's pregnant and I need my son to be alright. I know I wasn't a good man to her, but enough is enough. It's time for her to bring her ass home. If she would just answer her phone, then I'd be able to convince her to come home. I wonder if she stopped by Stacy's place? The last time I saw Stacy was that morning I shoved my Glock in her man's mouth. As I think about it now, that was some funny shit. I love to see niggas act like the bitches they are. Yeah! I'm the man, but I think it's time for me to make another surprise visit.

I dial Cee-Cee before I leave and of course, I get no answer. I jump in my ride and drive over to Stacy's house.

It's ten o'clock at night and Stacy's block is quiet. I pull up in front of her house and ring her doorbell. No one responds, but as I turn to walk away, I hear, "Who is it?" I come back up on the stoop and say, "It's me Tony. Can I talk to you for a minute?" The door unlocks and Stacy stands in the doorway with just a robe on.

"Hey! What's up Stacy?"

"Nothing! If you came here looking for Cee-Cee, she's not here and she won't be coming out this way anymore."

"Well, where she's at? Have you been talking to her?"

"Yeah, I've been talking to her, but I don't know where she's at. After that stunt you pulled with Spin, she felt responsible and she don't want me to get involved in her mess. She feels like it's safer if I don't know where she's at and she doesn't want to be found. She's alright though. If you want me to give her a message, I'll do that, but that's all I can do."

"Do you have a number where she can be reached?"

"Yeah, her cell. Her number is still the same. In fact, she gets all your messages. She just ain't picking up your calls."

"Yeah I know. I really fucked up huh? Do you think you can call her, so I can just hear her voice? I won't say a word. I just wanna hear for myself that she and my baby are alright. Talk to her on the speaker phone. I'll pay whatever you want."

"Don't destroy my friendship with Cee-Cee. I'll do this just one time and I'll tell you later how you can repay me

Stacy opens the door wider to let me in. I step in and follow her to her living room. The house is quiet, so I assume no one else is here. Well, not a nigga she's fucking. So, I lean back on the couch and wait for her to dial Cee-Cee's cell phone. As she turns on the speaker and Cee-Cee's phone rings loudly, I hear a sleepy voice say, "Hello." I could have died.

"What's up girl? Were you sleeping?" Stacy asks.

"Nah, I was watching TV. This baby got me tired and eating up shit. I'm not even showing, and I feel like I gained a hundred pounds."

"Aw! You sound so cute. I really wish I could see you and spend some time with you. I miss you Cee-Cee. I know you don't want to see Tony but he shouldn't stop you from seeing your friends."

"I know, but if I came to see you and Tony got wind of it, he'd be so angry. Besides, I'm at peace and I enjoy being by myself."

"Do you miss him?"

"Of course, I do but he's no good for me. I don't want anybody beating me up, damaging my face. That's not the kind of relationship I want. He is toxic."

"I know girl, but if you really love him, then you should try talking to him and work something out. I don't feel it's right for you to be raising a baby on your own when you don't have to."

"Well plenty of mothers do it every day, so it's no big deal. Anyway, enough about me and Tony. What's up with you?"

"Nothing. I just miss you and I hope I can be your baby's godmother."

"No doubt."

"Well, give me a call tomorrow, so we can chitchat. Get some rest."

"Aiight one."

While sitting there, listening to that whole conversation, I have mixed feeling. Some parts of me are happy because I've finally heard her voice. I needed to know that she and my son were alright but the other part of me is sad because I pushed away the woman I love. Cee-Cee is afraid of me and that's fucked up.

"So Tony, now that you've heard Cee-Cee's voice and heard for yourself that the relationship is over, what's up with me and you? I've been checking you out since the funeral, and I know you can lay it down."

Typical bitch. I knew Stacy was on my shit but I didn't think should would fuck her best friend's man. Now that she's showing me how grimy she is, I'll play this to my advantage.

"Stacy, I am a man that don't play games. You know I'm madly in love with Cee-Cee, but I'll hit your pockets up if you need help on anything."

"The only thing I need is that big, fat dick in my chocolate zone. I know you can fuck and I want some of that."

"Oh! So, you are a bold bitch. If I give you what you want, then you got to bring Cee-Cee to me."

"Now, how the fuck am I supposed to do that?"

"Well, do you want this fat, expensive dick? If you do, then you'll do whatever it takes."

I unzip my zipper and pull my dick out of my pants. I tell her to come and hold it. She walks over, grabs my cock and gently squeezes it.

"Damn! This pipe is heavy," she says and licks her lips.

I untie the knot on her robe and open it up a little bit. Stacy has a sexy style with a deep, dark complexion. She's aiight.

"I don't usually fuck on the first date," I say. "But your lips look so good. I want you to kiss your newfound friend."

Immediately, she obeys. Stacy gets on her knees and places tiny, little kisses all over my dick. To be honest, it feels uncomfortable disrespecting Cee-Cee, especially with her friend, but her friend ain't shit and I wanna bust this nut. I grab the back of her head and say, "Suck it. don't make love to it. Just suck it."

Stacy opens her mouth, and I force my big dick down her throat. She starts choking and gagging and I shake my head. She definitely can't suck dick like Tasty. This shit is already turning me off. Why bitches always wanna fuck somebody else's man, but can't fuck or suck for shit? Instantly, my dick gets soft. She looks at me and with pleading eyes and asks, "What's wrong?"

"Yo! I'm just stressing right now. I know you wanna have a good time, but I'm in my feelings. Maybe, I'll stop by here tomorrow, and we can pick up where we left off."

"Don't do that, Tony. Don't leave. Let's have some fun now. Whatever you wanna do, I'm down for it. I like you, so let me show you how much."

Stacy comes up off her knees, takes her robe off, puts my dick between her legs and grinds on it. I see she really wants this dick. She looks so sick and pitiful.

"Stacy, you have any condoms?"

"No baby. We don't need those. I like it raw. Skin-to-skin, flesh-on-flesh is the best sex."

Now, my dick really can't get hard. I would never stick my dick in none of these bitches raw.

"Yo, Yo, Yo! If you want this dick tonight, you are gonna go get some condoms. I don't fuck without them. So, stop grinding on me trying to get my dick hard and go get the shit. Time is ticking and I only have an hour to spare."

Stacy runs her ass up her stairs, gets dressed and flies out the door. I sit on her sofa, pick up her phone and dial the love of my life.

Chapter Twenty-Five

Bitches Ain't Shit

While I am laying in my bed dozing off and watching TV, my cell rings. SHIT! Who the fuck could this be at this time of night? I look at the name on my cell and it's Stacy again. What the fuck is up with her? She just called me a half hour ago. Anyway, let me answer.

"What's up girl?"

"What's up Tasty?"

Oh, my fucking God! How could Stacy set me up like this? My heart is beating one hundred miles per hour and I can't breathe.

"Tony!"

"Oh baby. It's so good to hear your voice. I miss you."

"Tony...I can't talk to you. Is Stacy there with you?"

"Tasty, don't worry about Stacy. She don't know I am making this call to you. Right now, I need you to hear what I got to say. What you're putting me through ain't right. I know I fucked up and I'm sorry. I'm so sorry baby, and I need you to come home so we can talk this thing out. I deserve another chance. I need you, I love you and I'm empty without you."

"Tony, I need you to just be easy. I wrote all that I had to say in my letter, and that's it. I don't know how you conned my friend into calling me, but I'll deal with her later. You hurt me Tony and I can't get with you. I'm pregnant and happy, so let me be."

"Tasty, I'm miserable. It's not fair that you are keeping my baby away from me. I wanna grow with the both of y'all and bond from conception. Baby, I love you. Doesn't that count for something?"

"Tony, I don't want to have this conversation. By the way, where is Stacy?"

"You know what? I said I was sorry a dozen times and you ain't trying to hear me. So, I see I'm a have to take drastic measures. Since you're so concerned about your whore-ass friend, I'm a show you she ain't shit and SHE will pay for your stubbornness."

"What the fuck are you talking about?"

"Just don't hang up. Listen and fucking learn. You need a reminder of who the fuck I am."

Tony continues babbling on and on, then he gets silent. All I can do is stay quiet and listen to him vent. Why the fuck Stacy got him over there is beyond me, but I'm a curse her ass out and drop her like a bad habit. While I'm sitting here getting my think on, I hear Stacy's voice in the background say, "I'm back and it's time to fuck the night away."

I freeze in silence and whisper, "Did I hear correctly? Is Stacy about to fuck Tony?" I listen on and connect my cell to my speaker box, so I can hear clearly. Really, I am hoping this is not about to go down. My friend trying to fuck my baby's father. That is some shiesty shit. As I sit up on the bed, I hear Tony say, "Stacy, I don't think it's right for you to ride my dick. You already know that no matter what, Cee-Cee is my wife."

"I don't want to hear about Cee-Cee. Tonight, it's all about me and you. Once you put that dick in my pussy, I'm a show you who the wife should be."

My ears ache. My heart splits and my eyes are watery. Bitches ain't shit and niggas are dogs. Why the fuck would he wanna fuck her? I know my pussy is sweeter and my head game is out of this world. Even if I had thought about getting back with him, that shit is dead now. Fuck them! But, I can't resist keeping my antennas up on the speaker.

I hear Tony say, "Give me the condoms. Strip butt ass naked and dance for me. Turn me on, bitch. You say you wanna fill Cee-Cee's spot? Then, show me what you got, but I must warn you. I'm a man that don't play games."

"Tony, I'm a give it all to you, and I guarantee you won't regret it," Stacy says.

"Oh yeah! Well, make that ass clap. Like that. Turn around. Now crawl to me like a dog and suck my dick better than that shit you did before. Cee-Cee takes every bit of my ten-inch-deep down her throat. Top that if you wanna walk in my wife's shoes."

Chapter Twenty-Six

Stacy's Horror

Speaking to Cee-Cee feels so good. Even though she is surprised and has a lot of anger towards me, it is still a pleasure to have her on the phone. I practically beg her to forgive me, but her throat won't let her speak. I'm sorry she feels this way, but because of her resentment, I have to be very cruel. I have to show her that her friend ain't shit and that I'm not the one to fuck with. Right now, I got her on hold. I want her to hear everything that's gonna take place tonight.

As I turn the speaker box up, Stacy walks into the house. She's all happy n' shit, but little does she know, this is going to be her worst nightmare. Tasty is on the phone listening and I know she is in disbelief. But hey, she calls Stacy her friend and I have to show her different. I told that bitch to hand me the condoms, strip, dance and crawl to me. Of course, she obeys. This bitch better suck sparks out of my dick. I pull my dick out and it's hard as a rock. I guess it's because Cee-Cee is on the on the phone listening. I grip the back of Stacy's hair and bounce my dick on her lips.

I say, "You see how hard it is now? I want all of this down your throat. Don't choke and no teeth. Suck the head of my dick and make it glisten with your spit."

I spread my legs a part a little and watch her suck my head. Now that I'm more relaxed, the suction is feeling good.

She says, "Does that feels good daddy?"

"Yeah," I say. "You is a nasty hoe. Why do you wanna suck Cee-Cee's dick? Huh? Do you know you got Cee-Cee in tears right now? She loves this dick and you're sucking the dick she loves."

I pull my dick out of her mouth real fast and slap her with it. She looks up and says, "What's wrong baby. You don't need to reminisce on someone who doesn't love or want you. I'm here now."

"Shut the fuck up and put my dick back in your mouth. Suck this dick slut, and deep throat it. If you don't, I'm going to punish you."

I hold the side of her head and work my dick in her mouth. I'm only four inches in and she's resisting my cock. I hold her head tighter, damn near pop her eyes out of her head and try to force the rest of my dick in her, but she gags. I'm so frustrated and mad that I slap the shit out of her ass for pretending she was that bitch. Stacy holds the side of her face with tears in her eyes and I hear an, "OH SHIT!" from the speaker phone. I walk over to the phone and say, "Cee-Cee, if you don't come to me, I'm going to kill this bitch tonight!"

Stacy says, "Oh my God! What did you say? You have Cee-Cee listening to us?"

"Yeah hoe! Cee-Cee is listening, scared to death and afraid for your life. You better beg for your life bitch and hope she comes to me. Now get the fuck up and suck this dick again. Deep throat it bitch and don't try to bite it."

Stacy cries and yells to Cee-Cee for help, but Cee-Cee doesn't say a word. She's just listening. I tell the bitch to get up and deep throat my hard-ass dick and make me cum. She looks at me with pleading eyes, and in a shaky voice says, "I can't. Please stop. Please don't hurt me."

Why the fuck she ain't get up? I hate a disobedient bitch. I walk up to her, grab her by her throat and start punching the shit out of her face. Screams from the speaker bring me back to reality. Cee-Cee is begging me to spare Stacy's life. I look down at this broad and her face is demolished. She is spitting up blood and a couple of teeth are missing.

"Cee-Cee, you got me deranged right now. This bitch is badly beaten because of you. All you got to do is tell me where you're at and let me come get you."

"Please Tony! Keep her out of this. I can't live with blood on my hands. I'm not coming home, so beating her to death is not going to change anything."

"Don't you hear her cries? Well, I guess they're not loud enough. Stay tuned and listen to this."

I walk back over to this bitch and say, "I'm a give you what you want. You love dick? Other people's dick. Well, bend over."

I turn Stacy over onto her stomach. She is so weak from her beat down that she can't even move. I stroke my dick a couple of times to get it semi-hard, put a condom on it and rub my dick up against her ass. Since she can't make me cum by giving me head, then I'm gonna bust this nut up in her ass. I position myself behind her, spread her ass cheeks and grin at her virgin asshole. I love a virgin asshole.

"Yo Cee-Cee!" I scream. "Stacy got a nice, virgin asshole. You know what it feels like to be fucked in it for the very first time and I was gentle with you. Listen to what it sounds like when there's no love or mercy."

I take my left hand to hold her cheeks apart and guide my dick into her ass. I feel my dick rip through her flesh, and she screams as I enter her. Her fingernails grip her carpet as I pump my fat dick inside of her. Cee-Cee is yelling and crying on the speaker, cursing me out something terrible, but I don't stop. This tight asshole works me into a frenzy. My balls are tingling and I'm about to explode. I got two females screaming and crying in my ear and it's bringing me to this ultimate pleasure. I thrust my dick deeper and harder. Then, I bust a crazy ill nut. I cum so hard that the condom blows up like a little balloon in her ass. I pull out and walk back over to the phone and say, "Cee-Cee, see what you made me do? If you would have done what I'd asked you to do, all of this could have been avoided. So now, my question to you is…should I keep her alive or should I kill this bitch? Right now, the decision is yours. You've got minutes to answer. I'm a wash my dick and when I get back, I want an answer."

I walk to the bathroom and handle my business. After fixing myself up, I can't help but smile. Tasty is coming home. I can feel it. I walk back to the living room and see Stacy still lying there, fucked up. I step over her and go to the phone.

"Okay! I'm back now. So, what's it's going to be?"

"KILL THE BITCH! Do whatever the fuck you gotta do? She disrespected the game anyway and I'll be damned if I come back to you. You are a sick muthafucka. We don't need you."

CLICK!

"This fucking bitch!" I scream.

I walk over to Stacy, grab a nice chunk of her hair and slice her fucking throat. I pick up everything that belongs to me and bounce.

While driving like a lunatic back to the house, my heart becomes evil. Whenever I find Cee-Cee, I will punish her ass, pregnant or not. No mercy for no one. It's on.

Chapter Twenty-Seven

Surprise Visit

I can't believe Tony raped Stacy. Even though she was all for it in the beginning, she still didn't deserve no shit like that. My heart goes out to her. I know she disrespected me, but fo-real, that's all a part of the game. I can't expect her to be one hundred when she is really fifty. I don't understand how she could put herself in that predicament, knowing that this muthafucka is crazy. Was the dick so important that she ignored the risks? I told her how dangerous he was, but she didn't listen. Tony is sick and demented. Yes…I, too fell for the dick, but after he put his hands on me and sodomized me, I knew I had to get the fuck out of there. It was just a matter of time before he would have killed me. WOW! I can't believe how this shit went down. Every time I think about it, tears well up in my eyes and I get numb. I hope he didn't kill her but I won't call to find out. I guess I'll tune into the news tomorrow. Right now, I'm a lay it down and pretend this shit didn't happen.

I wake up with a headache and a queasy stomach. It's hard for me to move around. I lay here for a minute to get my mind right and to also pray that Stacy is alright. Slowly getting up, I rush to the bathroom and throw up everything that is in my stomach. Being pregnant is the worst. I hate this morning sickness. After washing up and getting myself together, I decide to fix a big breakfast. I need to put back everything I just threw up and more. I make me some French toast, scrambled eggs with cheese, green peppers, onions and ham beef link sausages, English muffins, a fruit salad with cool whipped topping, a tall glass of water and orange juice. Yeah! That's what I'm talking about. I know my baby is going to be big and strong. I just hope it doesn't have Tony's unhealthy, bad ways.

As I sit and eat damn near all this food, I turn on the TV and debate if I should watch the news. I really don't want to see something on it that would spoil my day. I stand up, give Pus-Pus the rest of my food and walk to my porch. I breathe the cool, fresh air that is coming at me. The Fall is here so it's time to buy a whole new wardrobe, especially since I'm pregnant and getting fatter. Even though the morning sickness is killing me, the motherhood is going to be lovely. I can't wait.

I walk back into the house and stroll to the sitting room. I turn the TV on and flip through the channels. Nothing is really on, so of course, I tune into the midday news. I guess I'm just curious to see if Tony really is that crazy. As the news comes on and shows all these different shits I didn't want to see, I switch the channel to another program and something catches my attention. A reporter is saying something about seven brutal murders and before I can get the whole story, the reporter says, "We'll be back right after these messages." This shit goes to commercial and I panic. I pray and hold Pus-Pus tightly in my arms, hoping these are not my people I'm about to hear about. I'm scared. When the news comes back on, I pay close attention.

The special report comes on and the reporter is standing in front of Stacy's house and my heart stops. I knew she was dead. The reporter says, "The victim was raped, beaten and her throat was sliced." I cry hysterically and scream, "Why? Why the fuck did she put herself in that situation? Is this my fault? Should I have just went back to Tony and save her life? Why, why, why?" I ask myself all these questions and still come up with the same thing. She brought this on herself. Oh, God! This is horrible. I am definitely staying out of sight. Tony is going to kill me and I know he is out to get me. Fuck! C-note and Brother better get that furlough and handle my problem. Tony deserves to be mutilated and I wanna be right there when it happens. While I'm thinking on some crazy murderous shit, I notice that another reporter is in front of this strip club named, "Have it Your Way," and there's police tape around the joint. What the fuck? That's Tim-Tim's shit.

As I listen on, they say, "Tim-Tim and his five-man crew were violently murdered by a group of women known as *the Bronx Stick Up Chicks*. They all died from gunshot wounds to the backs of their heads. If anyone has any knowledge about these murders, please notify us immediately."

After hearing this shit, I got stuck on stupid. Too much shit is going down and it's scary. Who the fuck are these girls? These bitches have been doing some serious damage and niggas are still being careless. If they would have just gone home to their wives or girlfriend, they would still have their lives today. Damn! What a shame.

As I turn off the TV and walk back upstairs, my phone rings. I jet to my bedroom and answer it. It's Buddy.

"Hey Buddy, what's up?

"Nothing, what a gwan?"

"Good things. Are you still coming to see me?"

"Of course! Get up and let me in."

"What? You're here?"

"Open the door, baby girl."

I jet my ass down the stairs, open the door, run into Buddy's arms and bawl hysterically. Buddy stands there and holds me, trying to comfort me, but I am out of control. When he finally helps me regain my composure, we walk in and sit in the living room. I continue to cry a lot more as I tell Buddy the truth and nothing but the truth. By the time I finish explaining from the beginning to the end of Stacy's murder, we are three hours deep into our conversation. Buddy is totally disgusted and outraged. Of course, he blames me for all of this because, when Tony pushed up on me the first time, he should've been murdered. I played with a psycho and now he's out for blood.

"What am I gonna do, Buddy?"

"We hav feh kill him dead."

"Brother and C-note said they will handle this on their furlough."

"So yu wan feh wait til den? How long it gah tek feh get dis furlough?"

"As soon as they get to camp, so give it three months from now."

"Wha? Yu wan dis mon feh live three more months? Wha if he finds yu?"

"He won't. No one knows about this place. He knows I got a connect but he thinks I'm a two-bit hustler. He would never think about coming to the Hamptons. This is too big for him."

"Well, me nah trust him an I don't feel we should wait. He did too much damage an he need tah die now."

"Please Buddy, let's wait for Brother and C-note. They wanna deal with this."

"Cee-Cee, I hope yu nah protect dis mon. Me ah gah wait til deh furlough an after dat…ah dead him dead."

"Okay, so what brought you here this quick? I wasn't expecting you till next month."

"Well five hundred kilos yu get from me, so me wan feh see de money."

"Oh Buddy! You don't believe that Cee-Cee is handling her business? Huh?"

"Yeah, but me jus wan feh mek sure Tony didn't con yu out of we money."

"Alright then, follow me to my new vault."

I walk Buddy to his room. Yes, Buddy has his own room here. Every time he comes to New York, he stays with me. Buddy is also very secretive. He never lets anyone know when he's coming. At least, not the day of. Buddy also knows the security code, but he never uses it. One time, he caught C-note and I doing a sixty-nine and ever since that, he would call outside of the house for us to let him in. If no one answers, then he will use the security code to let himself in.

We enter his room and he put his bags up. I take him to the linen closet, remove a piece of carpet from the corner and show him the numeric keypad. The security code is B-U-D-D-Y. I enter his name, and the wall with the towels moves. We step in and Buddy is amazed to see the $3.7 mill neatly stacked. I tell him all about Danny and how I gave him the first shipment on consignment and how, two weeks later, all the money was sent to me through Pete. I let him know that I gave him another shipment on consignment and that money should be coming sometime next month. Buddy is very impressed and I am ecstatic.

"Well baby girl, me see yu ah handle yah business even bettah den yah brother and C-note."

"Nah, I found the right guy who needs our product 'cause he has a lot of people to supply. This nigga is on the map now. He's got crazy spots and knows mad people. I'm glad I took the chance. He's definitely the man."

"Yeah I see. Well another reason why me come is because me have some people who ah work some airport business feh me. Big tings ah gwan feh we, an since me see yu can handle dah pressure, den let's overdo it and get out. At least, by the time Brother and C-note get home, we can start our legit business."

"Yeah, I'm with that, but remember, my people can only handle 250-300 keys at a time."

"Well, me ah gah tell Pete he have feh find another big distributor. He ah gah tell Danny dat his keys are now twelve gees and the new guy fifteen. We can more than afford feh lower if me ah get boat shipment at one hundred gees a shipment. The people in Venezuela are really good to me, an me done tell them me a stop next year. Dem nah mind 'cause dey hav some big key players innah England who ah triple wha me a get, so walking out is no big ting. Me ah gah meet up with Pete tonight an introduce him to the baggage handler and three air stewardess who work feh American Airlines. He doesn't have to recruit no more girls. The air stewardess ah gah put da suitcase through and bring it here an he will meet dem. These new people on our team will bring nuff drugs. Each suitcase will have fifty keys and the beauty about it is that they can fly in and out of the country whenever they wan without any suspicion. We also ah gah buy another storage spot to hold all these drugs. Pete hav feh really work now and all you hav feh do is collect deh money."

"My only concern about this is...are you sure the people in Venezuela is going to let you get out?" Even though they have other key players, you are they big man on this side."

"Every ting cool. Trust me."

"Everything sounds good, so let's get it on and popping."

While sitting there talking about our plans for the future, my cell phone rings. I walk over and look on the ID and it's Tony. I walk back over to Buddy and show him the name. He snatches the phone and answers it.

"Hey pussyhole. Yu is one dead mon."

"Who the fuck is this? Who the fuck is answering my muthafucking wife's phone?"

"One of yah biggest nightmares, pussy."

"Oh yeah?"

"Yah."

"Where the fuck is Cee-Cee?"

"Yu will never see Cee-Cee again. Not in this lifetime. When me find yah bloodclatt, me ah gah clap some heat inna yah ras."

"Listen, you Jamaican ass…"

"Pussy. Me ah no Jamaican. Me is ah cool and deadly mon who gah skin yah ras alive. All yu bad bwoy wan feh put yah han pon dah women and afraid ah real mon. But me ah gah show yu star. So, yu bettah run bwoy. Run far cause me ah gah kill yu."

CLICK!

Buddy turns to me and says, "Don't worry 'bout him. Soon, he will find out."

We continue to talk some more. Then I retire to bed. I leave him, and he gets himself ready to make his moves.

Chapter Twenty-Eight

Breakthrough

It's been six months since I've seen Tasty. She won't answer her cell, and she's fucking some fake-ass Jamaican dude. I can't believe she would let some weak ass muthfucka slide up in her, knowing I'm the only one that can make her feel how she wanna feel. She played herself big time. All I wanna do is find her. I can't say what I'll do to her but she needs to be taught a lesson. I thought she would have come to her senses when she learned about her friend's death but she didn't. She didn't even come to Stacy's funeral. That surprised me. I was there giving my condolences like I was hurt by it but I was really looking for her. What is crazy is how over a hundred niggas showed up, went up to Stacy's mom and introduced themselves like, "I'm her man." What a slut! I'm glad Cee-Cee didn't follow in her footsteps cause as they say, birds of a feather flock together, but Cee-Cee has her own mind. Damn! I miss her. I wonder how she's doing with her pregnancy. I should be there rubbing her stomach, letting my son know I'm there. Well, she's missing out. I should be giving her the world right now. Since I'm the man now, she would have loved what I have to offer. I am the head nigga in charge. New York is fucked up and in distress. Half of the OGs are dead, and the other half are starving. I'm the last man standing with no heart. No one can eat unless I say so. If any drugs are being dealt, it's gotta come through me. Since I'm the only man with the keys to supply, the stakes went up to twenty-five gees a pop. No consignments, no breaks, no nothing and only my drugs run through the streets of NY. Anyone gets caught selling shit that ain't mine is dead. Yeah! I control this muthafucka.

When I was the little nigga, I was the one making runs for everybody. I got a gee here and there and nobody would trust me with shit. I was only good for making drop offs and pick-ups but now, they got to come to me. Look how the tables have turned. I understand that they got some nigga in the South that's doing crazy business and that his connect is from NY. I don't know how that can be because I'm the only man standing. If I didn't know any better, I would have thought it was Cee-Cee because she got a strong connect, but one thing I do know, she doesn't have a distributor. That's why she dealt with me, so I know it ain't her. So, who is this person? I gotta find out, and I gotta find out how they are getting their drugs through. Cee-Cee jerked me with that connect, but it's all good because I'm still getting paid in full.

Cee-Cee is doing a good job staying out of sight. I put a price on her head for a hundred grand. She's not to be hurt. I just want her location and I'll take it from there. The fucked-up thing is, nobody knows this girl and the only information I can give out is the name Cee-Cee. Is that her real name or what? I don't even know. I had niggas posted up at Brother and C-note's jails for months and she never showed up. I am so frustrated. I feel sorry for every bitch who is on my shit. I fuck them, beat them and then kill them. Bitches don't understand that I'm in my feelings. Cee-Cee's got my heart and I'm fucked up over her. I need her. Every time I think about her, my dick gets rock hard. I pick up my phone to dial her cell and of course, no answer. I roll a blunt, smoke it, and sip on some Hennessey. The weed instantly penetrates my brain. I climb upstairs, feeling high and sad and plop my ass on my bed. I take my clothes off, strip and continue getting high.

While looking up at the ceiling, my mind is on Cee-Cee. I look down to reach the ashtray and notice my dick is at full attention. I lay in Cee-Cee's spot and put my dick in my hand. I close my eyes and picture Cee-Cee in my head. As I imagine every good and sweet thing about her, I stroke my dick. It's two in the morning and I need to make love to Cee-Cee. I pick up my phone and dial Cee-Cee. The phone rings. I am so shocked when I hear the sweetest voice I've ever known say, "Hello."

Chapter Twenty-Nine

Head Sprung

Climbing up the stairs is the worst. I'm fat, wobbly and tired. I don't understand how people can get pregnant three or four times and be happy. I am one miserable bitch and I can't wait to get this baby out of me. Last night, I almost cut a hole in my mattress to stick my belly in it. I hate sleeping on my side and back. I need to sleep on my stomach. This is too much. I am losing me, and I want my body back. Three more months to go and I don't know how I'm gonna make it.

C-note calls me every day. I've been sending him mad pictures of me and my developing stomach. He loves it and he's very anxious to be a dad. He and brother put in for their furloughs for my delivery. Since their time is so short, they were approved for seven days. I can't wait. I need them here. Not only for my pregnancy, but for the business. My position is limited now. I only collect money. Pete is up front and center and he is doing the damn thing. Danny is a blessing also. He is top dawg in the South and he is keeping my safe stacked. I love him. We also got a new guy named Stan. He is another official nigga. He buys weight and brings everything in full. I haven't met him, and I don't want to. Pete is the head nigga right now so I'm a let him shine. Besides, motherhood is knocking at my door, so I need to lean back. I'm glad Buddy got everything under control before he left. He spent a month with me and made sure everything is running smoothly. He is also coming back when Brother and C-note get their furloughs. All of us together…that is gonna be some shit. Boy I can't wait. I miss all of us being together as one. Besides, we need to help NY. Everyone over there is screaming for relief. Those Bronx bitches have done crazy damage. They have killed a lot of players, and the ones who are still alive are broke as hell. I feel bad for them, but that's how the cookie crumbles. Niggas should know to put money up for a rainy day, but in this drug game, niggas only live for today. So really, it's their bad.

I got wind a couple of months ago that Tony is the man in New York. That surprises me because he doesn't have a strong connect. So, who is his supplier? How is he the only one standing and the top dawg when he is a nobody? How the fuck did he climb up the ladder? Who knows, and who give a fuck. I also heard that he put a price on my head to find me. Silly nigga. He can't find me. I don't know why he's still trying. You would think he would have said, "fuck it," by now. I know it can't be the baby, so what is it? Plenty of times, I've been tempted to call him. I wanna hear his voice and I'm yearning to make love to him. If he wasn't a stupid-ass nigga, we could have been making love all this time. But hey, he blew it and I can't chance it. Tony calls me all the time, when I look at my cell and see his name, I don't answer. I don't know why I haven't changed my number. I guess I like the attention. Like now, he's ringing my cell. I'm afraid to answer. Really, I don't know what to say. I do wanna talk to him and I miss him. By the time I finish debating with myself, the phone stops ringing. I'm so frustrated. I walk my ass to the shower to cool off. I get out, dry off and lay my fat naked ass on my bed and reminisce on the past with Tony.

I hate thinking about Tony because when I do, my mind takes me there. I love C-note with everything I got, but there's something about Tony that got me fucked up. My nipples are hard right now, and my pussy is wet. Not to mention, the baby is kicking the shit out of me. I guess I got the baby's hormones up in rage because I'm in heat. As I lay here rubbing on my milky, firm breasts, my cell rings again. It's real late, so who could be calling? I look at my cell and with a smile on my face, I say, "Hello." It takes a couple of seconds for the voice to respond. I guess he's shocked that I answered.

"Tasty."

"Yeah."

"I can't believe you answered your cell. How are you doing? What's going on with the baby?"

"I'm fine, and so is the baby. What's going on with you?"

"Loving and missing you to death. Tonight, is the best night of my life. I can't believe I am talking to you."

"Yeah, well you are."

"Tasty, let's not argue. Since I got you on the phone, lets just stay on it for hours and catch up on everything. I need to know that you are alright. Do you have a big belly?"

"Man, I'm huge. I wobble when I walk, and I eat everything in sight. Sometimes, I wonder if I will ever get my shape back."

"Tasty, don't worry about that. You are a fine-ass woman and no matter what, I will always love you."

"Well, that's nice to know."

"Tell me something. Do you miss me?"

"Yes."

"Do you think about me?"

"All the time. I am carrying your child. How could I not."

"So, how come you never pick up on my calls? Why haven't you ever called me?"

"Because Tony, you are crazy. Look at what you did to me. You beat the shit out of me twice for no reason, and then you raided a spot that should not have been entered. How am I supposed to live with a man that keeps doing horrible shit to me? You did that craziness to Stacy, put me on the speaker phone to hear you torment her and you murdered her. Am I supposed to feel comfortable with you? You turned out to be a totally different nigga than the one I met three and half years ago?"

"Tasty, I'm extremely sorry for what I did to you. Ownership is what I believe in and I wanted to own every part of you from head to toe. In my eyes, you belong to me. From the first day, I met you I knew I had to have you and I prayed every night for you to look in my direction, but you never did. I respect that in you because it showed me that you're a dedicated woman, and I need someone like you by my side. I know you have strong feelings for C-note, but right now, that's not even an issue. You carrying my child is the issue. I need you. I need the family I started. I'm hurt, Tasty. Please don't deny me that."

"Tony, I can't come back to you. I'm afraid of you and I'm afraid for my life. I'll converse with you over the phone and keep you posted, but I can't and won't jeopardize me and my child's life."

"Tasty, I'll tell you what. Meet me in public. You don't have to come here. Let's go to dinner, see a movie and I'll put you in cab until the next time you want to see me again. Give me the benefit of the doubt. I want to show you my real love. I love you, Tasty and I'll die trying to make you happy. I know one day you will come home to me. Everything is how you left it and no woman has entered your home."

"You haven't brought any girls there?"

"Hell no! I'm not gonna say I'm innocent, but no one can get my heart. I love you and only you. So, tell me, what's going on with you and your Jamaican friend?"

"I don't have a Jamaican friend. He is a relative and he's very angry. He doesn't want you in my life and I have to honor his wish."

"Yeah, but you're having my baby and he also needs to respect that."

"Anyway, I'm tired. I need to get some rest. I'll call you tomorrow, so we can chat some more. I won't shut you down but take time with me."

"Alright, this is the beginning and I do appreciate you accepting my call. I love you and good night."

"Goodnight."

I hang up the phone, feeling all depressed and shit. I lay on my side and tears fall from my eyes. Why did I answer the phone? Why do I let him get to me? I miss him. I need him. I want him. After crying my eyes out for about twenty minutes, I decide to go and see him. I know I shouldn't, but he sounds so different and sincere. I don't think he will harm me, so I'm a take a chance. I get up and put on my oversized sweat suit and kicks. It's three o'clock in the morning, so I call a cab.

The cab will be here in fifteen minutes. I'm waiting for the cab so anxiously that I begin to get nervous, and before I can change my mind, the cab driver blows his horn. Damn! Fuck it! Be brave and go see what is really going down. I walk out of the house, get in the cab and pray everything works out fine. An hour-and-a -half to get to my destination and I can't wait to get there. Tony is going to be surprised.

Chapter Thirty

Fuck & Leave

The cab finally pulls up in front of Tony's house. I pay the man, get out and slowly walk up the walkway. I notice that my truck is still in the driveway and in front of it is a brand-new Lexus coupe. I can see he is really feeling himself. I walk to the stoop, stand at the door and ring the doorbell. I press the doorbell, at least six times, but he's not answering. I take out my cell and dial his phone. On the fifth ring, Tony picks up and says, "Whad up?"

"Nothing honey. It's me."

"Cee-Cee?"

"Yeah. Wha cha doing?"

"I was sleeping, dreaming about making love to you endlessly?"

"Would you like that?"

"More than you'll ever know."

"Well, come get me."

"Stop playing girl."

"Come get me and make love to me like I'm the only woman on this earth."

"Tasty, where are you? I'm coming now."

"Downstairs in front of the house."

Tony drops the phone and I hear him tumbling down the stairs. The door unlocks and when he opens the door, Tony is standing in the doorway butt-ass naked. He comes halfway onto the stoop and pulls me in. When he locks the door behind me, he stands there dumbfounded looking at me speechless. I walk up to him and take his hands and place them on my stomach and instantly the baby kicks. Tony looks at me and smiles. He gets on his knees, caresses my belly, feels it and kisses it. The amount of 'I love yous' that come out of his mouth are unbelievable and when he looks up at me, there are tears in his eyes. This moment is so sensitive and intimate that I start to cry. Tony gets up off his knees and holds me close. We stand on the porch, holding on to each other for dear life and for the first time, I feel safe in his arms. After standing for what seems like hours, Tony grabs my hand and escorts me upstairs.

When we get to our bedroom, he instantly turns me around and starts undressing me. I seductively watch him and help him get me out of my clothes. While we stand there in the nude, Tony admires my pregnant body. He touches me gently and lays me down on my side of the bed. Tony lays halfway on top of me, rests his head on my breasts and keeps his hands on my stomach. We lay and fall asleep without saying a word.

It's eleven o'clock in the morning and Tony's cell is ringing, so I answer it.

"Hello."

"Hello. Who the fuck is this?" some chick on the other line asks.

"Excuse me?"

"You heard me bitch! Who the fuck is this?"

"This is Cee-Cee. Now, who are you?"

"I'm Tony's girl, Wanda."

"Is that right?"

"Yeah. Now, where is my fucking man? Put him on the fucking phone."

"Sure hon. No problem."

I nudge Tony and as usual, his stubborn ass ignores me. I pinch him real hard and he whines, "Ouch."

"Tony, Wanda is on the phone for you. Can you please tell your girls not to disrespect me?"

"What? No females call this house Tasty."

"Well, there's one on the phone now."

Tony takes the phone and starts wilding the fuck out. He is so mad, all he says, "You should have never done this. Cee-Cee is my wife and the love of my life, and no one disrespects her. I'll see you later," and hangs up.

I lay there on my back and say to myself, "Tony is gonna hurt this girl." I feel sorrier for her than mad at her. In fact, I'm even scared for her life. Tony lays there in my arms, apologizing sincerely for what just went down. I accept and tell him to calm down. Tony looks at me, smiles and then caresses my stomach, real gentle and smooth. He works his way to my hot spot and brushes his hands against it and works his hands back up to my breasts. My nipples are so erect and tender, but they still want to be sucked. Tony holds one breast and puts it in his mouth. He sucks on my breasts like he is breastfeeding himself. It feels so good. The sensation has me freaked.

"Umm," I moan, letting him know I'm enjoying it. While he's sucking on my left breast, I am playing with the right. Tony has my left nipple crazy hard with a half inch erection. "Suck the other nipple," I moan. Tony leans over me and sucks the shit out of my right nipple. My head is so fucked up that I can't wait for the penetration. I've longed for this and now that I'm getting it, I'm going to satisfy my every need.

While holding the back of his head and letting him know that I'm enjoying this shit, Tony brings his face up to my face and tongues the shit out of me, making me feel good. Saliva is dripping all down my neck.

"Umm. I want more. Tony, make love to me," I moan.

Tony eases up off my nipple and goes down to my stomach. He kisses all over my belly. Then, he parts my legs. I open them up and watch his head get lower and lower until my stomach blocks my view. Tony kisses my pussy. He puts soft pecks all over it, teasing me. I wanna scream, "Just suck it!" but I don't. I let him take his time. Tony sticks his tongue in my moist hole and slowly tongue fucks me. I am so open. I can't stand it. While he tongue-fucks me, he puts his thumb on my clit and plays with my little bud.

"Oh Tony, I missed you."

Tony licks my pussy up to my clit and sucks on it until I scream, shake and cum. I cum so hard in his mouth, he just keeps sucking until I beg him to fuck me. Tony comes up on his knees, and when I look at him, his dick is so hard with pre-cum leaking from it.

"Turn around and put your ass in the air," Tony says. I turn around, put my ass in the air, spread my legs and feel what I've been longing to feel. God, this is gonna feel so good. "Are you ready for me?" Tony asks. I nod my head, letting him know I want it all. I wanna feel his stainless-steel penetration in my hole.

Tony presses his dick up against my sweetness and pushes his head inside. My pussy squeezes his dick like a vice grip and he moans out in ecstasy. I'm moaning too, 'cause the pleasure is so good, so right. Tony slowly works his dick in until he is ten inches deep. Then, he slowly pulls it back out, up to the head. He already knows that slow-motion fucks drive me crazy. I grind on his dick, showing my appreciation for having this wonderful cock inside of me. I also tighten up my pussy muscles, letting him know that he will never find a pussy as good as mine. Tony long dicks me, nice and gentle. He feels real good. As the second round of waves erupts in my body, Tony moans loudly. I know it's because he feels my hot cum all over his dick. Tony's dick is coated with my cream. Tony pulls his dick out, shoves his face in my ass and sucks my pussy from the back. He licks my pussy, giving me pleasurable head. Then, he rams his dick back inside of me, giving hard penetration. I grab a pillow and rock with his grinds. Yeah, it might have been a long time since I had some, but I gotta show him that I am still just as wicked and wild as ever. While I back my ass up on him and make it clap, Tony moans out of control. He spreads my butt cheeks, squeezes my butt cheeks and screams my name as he explodes. Tony fucks my pussy with the madness and drains his hard-ass dick in my pussy.

While I am still bent over, I tell him, "Take all of me. Let's this be a night we'll never forget."

Tony continues to pump, not understanding what I'm saying, so I reach to the back, pull his dick out and say, "Not in there...in here."

I point his dick to my asshole and Tony looks at me like, "What is up with you? Do you really want that?"

"If I didn't, I would not have said it. You want all of me? Then, ownership me with gentleness."

Tony gets off the bed, goes to the dresser and gets some K-Y Jelly. First, he greases up his dick and my asshole. Then, he works his middle finger inside. This shit is feeling so good that I can't help but moan. When he sees how I'm loving it, he puts two fingers inside of me. Tony pulls out his fingers and say, "I'm about to enter, so take a deep breath. I'm gonna be real gentle."

Tony puts the head of his dick at the entrance of my ass and gently pushes it in. I grab on to the pillows and call out his name through clenched teeth. Tony stops for a minute until my breathing is in control, and then slowly works his way in. Inch by inch, I feel his penetration and it is painful, but I'm not telling him to stop. In fact, I want all of it to go in, so we can really get into it. Tony is behind me, moaning all different types of things. He pushes in further and now six inches of him are inside of me. He stops and asks if I'm alright. By this time, my face is buried in the pillow, biting in the pillow, leaving deep teeth marks all over it with sweat beading off my forehead.

"Tasty, I'm not gonna put anymore in. I'm just going to work this spot right here. Just keep breathing and everything is gonna be alright. If you want me to stop just say so. I don't want to hurt you. I love you Tasty and right now, you got me above and beyond cloud nine."

"No baby don't stop. It hurts a lot, but I want you to do this. I love you and I just want you to make me feel good."

Tony pulls his dick back and rides inside again. Six inches of slow fucking is turning out to be the best fuck of my life. I start moving back on him and he slowly picks up the pace.

"More!" I scream. "Give it all to me."

Tony spreads my ass cheeks and climbs all the way in until he's in ten inches deep. He moans, I moan and his body jerks.

"Oh God! Tasty! You are blowing my mind. I'm cummin, mommy! I'm cummin."

Tony keeps his ten inches in my ass and lets out loads of hot, thick cum. As he finishes, his dick gets semi-hard. He doesn't pull it out. Instead, he works his dick in and out of me. The semi-hard dick feels so good. It's not too big and the k-y jelly makes the pain a whole lot more tolerable. As Tony works his dick inside my asshole, I bounce back on it, showing him that I enjoy it and want more. While his dick blossoms again, Tony's moans get louder. He spreads my legs wide and fucks my ass like a mad man. By now, the pain is more bearable because it's been worked in gently. Tony spares no mercy this time. He digs all up in my ass and thrusts powerful blows in it.

I cry, "Spank my ass, Tony! Spank it," and he does.

As he delivers tormenting thrusts to my ass, I feel the beginnings of powerful eruption inside of me.

"Tony?" I yell and he says, "Yeah Tasty, I feel you. This is an orgasm of a lifetime. Flow on my dick baby."

Tony reaches under me and starts playing with my clit. I try to push his hand away and he's not having it.

"Cum baby. Cum for me. Show me how much you miss me."

Tony thrust two more heavy hitters and then I cum all over the place. I cum so much and so hard I think I'm going to pass the fuck out. My body is so sensitive, and I want to stop, but Tony's dick is still rock hard. I know he won't stop. Tony flips over, lies on his back and tells me to ride him with his dick in my ass. I climb on top of him, push his dick back in my ass and squat on him. Tony screams out my name and reaches for my titties. He puts them in his mouth, squeezes both titties together and sucks the shit out of my nipples. We are both in heaven and loving every minute of it. I lean back on Tony's dick and stretch it outwards. I bend it, twist it, grind it and cream all over it. Tony is going crazy. His dick is about to explode. He leans up a little bit and puts his finger in my wet pussy. He fingers fucks my pussy, while his dick fucks my ass. Damn, that is a crazy sensation. I'm over the top. He calls my name and he cums all in my ass. I roll off Tony and lay in his arms like a baby. He cradles me and holds me tight.

He says, "I'll never let you go, and I'll never hurt you again."

I believe him, but the saddest part is I gotta leave him.

For the next three days, Tony and I love each other down. We stay in the house and do us. Tony takes very good care of me, and he is really proud and ecstatic that I am pregnant. On the third day, Tony tells me that he has something planned for me that night. He says that he's gonna make some runs and that he'll be back at eight. Tony gets dressed and leaves. As soon as he's gone, I take a nice, hot shower, straighten up, get dressed and walk to the train station. I take the train to 34th Street in Manhattan and get on the Long Island Railroad back to the Hamptons. I take this long route to be on the safe side. I know when Tony gets back home and discovers that I am gone, his heart is gonna be broken. He loves me, but I'm not leaving C-note.

Chapter Thirty-One

Last Conversation

By the time I return to Yepton Mansion, I am exhausted. I lay down on the couch with wobbly legs and sore thighs. Even though I feel the way I do, it was all worth it. I needed my body to be fucked right. Besides, I loved the anal sex. That shit was mind blowing.

C-note is gonna be mouth, pussy and ass whipped when he comes home. He ain't gonna be able to understand, but he's gonna love it when I take control. C-note got a bad ass dick, too, but he's not as experienced. There's a lot of freaky shit I wanna get into and he better be down. Speaking of C-note, what explanation am I gonna give him for why he hasn't heard from me for last three days. I better think of something real fast, because he ain't trying to hear no shit about Tony. Oh, poor Tony. He is going to go ape shit. What a shame. I wish things could be different but they can't be, so it don't make sense to cry over it. I'm not gonna wait for him to call me. I'm gonna call him and tell him how I feel.

I walk my lazy ass up the stairs to my room and strip down. I put my robe on, take out my cell and dial Tony. He immediately picks up and asks, "Baby, where are you?"

"Are you home yet?" I ask him.

"I'm here now, and you're not here. Where are you?"

"Tony, we need to talk. I don't want you getting upset. I want you to understand. First, let me say, the last three days were wonderful. I wish you could have made me feel that way in the beginning. Being in your arms and making sweet, passionate love to you was all that I could ask for. I love you Tony, but we can't be as one. I'm sorry if I hurt your feelings, and even sorrier for picking up the phone, but I

163

did, and I enjoyed what we shared."

"Tasty! You are fucking with my head. How are you gonna just up and leave and expect me to be alright with this? I don't like you. I love you. I'm in love with you Tasty. A part of me is growing inside of you every day. You can't shut me out, especially after I made all those promises to you. Don't hurt me like this, Cee-Cee. Please don't. Come home and let's talk about it and get past this. Yo, I'm fucked up for real. Tears are in my eyes and my heart is bleeding."

"Tony I can't. I already made plans for my future. The baby and I are going to be alright and I'll keep you posted. If it's gonna be too hard for you to speak to me from time to time, then I'll understand. I love you, but I can't be with you. You almost had me. Your charm and firm approach is what got me hooked, not to mention your sex appeal, but I have a life, a life you would never understand or know anything about. Go on and live your life. Maybe, you should consider Wanda as your woman. She seems like a nice girl."

"Don't play with me. I don't want no fucking Wanda. In fact, Wanda doesn't exist anymore and it's not about her, it's about you. I love you. Please come home and let's be a family. All I need is me, you and our newborn baby. I'm sick right now and this is gonna cause major problems. I'm gonna find you. If you don't come home and I find you, this will be very bad for you. That I promise."

"Tony, I got to go. Take care and get over me."

"Wait."

CLICK!

I lay in my bed and cry my eyes out. Why the fuck did I go there? It's too late to turn back the clock now.

Chapter Thirty-Two

Tony's Informant

That's twice I got burned by this bitch, but this time was the worst. I feel used and abused. Fucked and dumped. Is that all I'm good for? I should have known. For months, Cee-Cee doesn't answer her phone, then out of the blue at two o'clock in the morning she picks up. The conversation we had was pleasing and it gave me hope that she would come around. I was open and when we hung up, I fell asleep like a baby dreaming about her. Two hours later, I am awakened by her cell, telling me to open the door. I could not believe my ears or eyes when I saw Cee-Cee standing there. That was the happiest moment of my life…seeing Cee-Cee with a nice, round belly, plump and looking motherly. I fell more in love. We made love for three lovely days, and she gave me all of her willingly. That blew my mind. I never thought, in a million years, after what happened, that she would let me dig in that ass again, but she did. That was the bomb. I just knew everything was everything, but know looking back on shit, and how everything went down, Cee-Cee used me. The pregnancy got her hot in the ass and she used my body to satisfy her needs. I enjoyed every minute of it, but that's all she wanted…to lead me on and make me think she was home for good and that's fucked up. I'm hurt, sad and out of control. After she left, she calls me that night, telling me some bullshit. How the fuck is she gonna tell me we can't be together? Come on now. She's carrying my seed. I can't just let her go. What kind of man would I be? I told her I'd find her, and I will. I got someone working on that right now. When I do find her, I will not have mercy on her. She's a little bitch and she needs to be taught a lesson. I am sick and tired of playing these little games with her. I am a grown-ass man and I need a real woman in my life. If she can't provide that for me, then I'll understand. Just give my son or daughter to me and keep it moving. That's my first and I want it. I'll raise the baby on my own. Plus, I got mad family who wouldn't mind helping me do this. I deserve to be a part of my child's life, so I have to find her. She's good though, and once again, my dumbass didn't get her information. I guess I was so overwhelmed at having her home that I didn't think she was going to leave. It's all good though. I have faith this time on locating her. Niggas are hungry, and they want this loot, so they will have some information for me. One thing I am glad for though is that she is picking up on my calls now, but the bullshit about everything is that it's on her time. I'll handle whatever she dishes out. I just hope she can do the same.

As I am getting ready to leave the house, my cell phone rings. I don't know who this person is and the name and number don't look familiar, but I'll answer. "Yo! Who dis?"

"It's Chicago nigga."

"What's the deal? You got something for me?"

"Yeah. You need to get at me ASAP. Meet me at this Jamaican restaurant called *Wicked.* It's on Farmers and Linden in Queens. You know that spot?"

"Hell yeah! I eat there all the time."

"I'll be there in an hour."

"Cool."

"One."

I click this nigga off and pray that he's got some good shit for me. This is the nigga who is supposed to be looking for Cee-Cee. If this is what I think it is, then Cee-Cee is in for the shock of her life. I told her I was going to find her.

I get my shit ready, smoke a crazy big blunt and walk out the door. This is going to be an interesting day. While I'm cruising to *Wicked,* I decide to call Cee-Cee. She picks up and answers with a tired voice, but it sounds so sexy.

"Hey Tony."

"Hey momma."

"What's going on?"

"Nothing. I was just thinking about you, so I decided to give you a call. You know I got to check on my two babies."

"Yeah, I know."

"Anyway, I just wanted to hear your voice. You know I love you and I'm praying every night that you will come to your senses and come home. I do believe God will answer my prayers real soon."

"Well, let's not get into that. What is meant to be will be."

"True dat! Well, I'ma holla at you later, so stay tuned."

I hang up without letting on that I will be seeing her real soon because, little does she know, it is about to be on and popping.

I pull up in front of *Wicked* and walk in. Chicago is sitting at a table by the window. He puts up his hand. I walk over and sit down. One of the waitresses comes over and I order a plate of oxtails, rice n' peas, yellow plantains and a salad. For my drink, I get a large carrot juice. I also tell her to bring me a shot of Hennessey. Something tells me I'm a need more than a stiff drink, but this will have to do for now.

"So, Chicago! What's the deal son?"

"Yo! I know you wanna find your girl Cee-Cee, but I don't have her location."

"So, what the fuck you call me for?"

"I got someone just as good. Cee-Cee was seen yesterday with this nigga named Pete. They were hugged up and he was all over her stomach. Pete is the nigga who is supplying the whole South. He is larger than large. In fact, he is larger than you. Nobody knows about this nigga because he is low key, but he is the man. From my understanding, this is Cee-Cee's new man. They have been seen together quite a few times."

"WHAT? This is definitely interesting. Do you know where this Pete lives?"

"Yeah! He lives in Jamaica Estates in a big fucking house."

"Okay. Is he there all the time?"

"Nah, mainly at night. Do you want me to handle this situation?"

"Oh no! You did good son. Real good. I know everything I need to know. This is something I have to handle myself. Tonight, call me with the exact address of this Pete and tomorrow I'll meet you back here with a hundred bands. You did good son. Real good."

Chapter Thirty-Three

Pete's House

I left the fucking restaurant mad as shit. Cee-Cee did the damn thing…no correction! Cee-Cee is doing the damn thing. How could I be so fucking stupid? I should have known Cee-Cee is that bitch. That top dawg bitch. It all makes sense. She played me well. I'm supposed to be the last man standing, but instead, I got a bitch on top of me. My fucking baby's momma at that. Here I'm thinking this bitch is broke and suffering and needs my help and she done outdid a nigga. What a bitch! When I get hold of her, I'm going to squash her like a bug. She better hope she makes it through this shit. I'm at the point now that I don't even give a fuck about the baby. Is it even my baby? She got me wondering. Maybe, it's this nigga Pete's kid. Well, it's over for him. New York is my city and he should not be moving anything from this side. I got something for him. Cee-Cee should have told him that I am a crazy-ass nigga. If he doesn't know, he will soon find out. Not to mention, he is sliding up in my pussy. I will cut his dick off and shove it in his mouth. He will pay for Cee-Cee's bullshit.

As I drive at top speed to my house, anxiety takes full control over me. I have never been this anxious about killing a nigga before, but I am. These muthafuckas played me. I feel like the biggest fool ever.

I pull up in my driveway and jet into the house. I run upstairs and count out a hundred bands for this nigga Chicago and wait for his call. I roll a blunt and snatch a bottle of Henny off the bar and put it to the head. I drink and smoke for hours, mean-mugging in the mirror. I even start talking to myself. That' how mad I am. All types of crazy shit is filling my head and my thoughts are all the same and that's, "KILL THOSE MUTHAFUCKAS!" Pete is going to get it so bad that he's gonna tell me where Cee-Cee's at. He would be a fool not to. He's going to die anyway. As I keep entertaining these thoughts in my head, my cell rings interrupting me. I pick it up. It's Chicago. He gives me the address to Pete's house. I write it down and tell him to meet me at *Wicked* tomorrow at one. I hang up and stare at the address. I blow smoke on it and say, "You are one dead nigga. Your days are numbered."

While I continue smoking and drinking, a deep sleep comes over my eyes.

Wow! I must have passed out because it's noon and I'm just waking up. I shower, dress and jet out the door to meet Chicago. I cruise to *Wicked* and a make a quick drive past Pete's house. I sit across the street and stare at it. It's a beige and white tri-level house with a three-car garage. In the driveway, there is a 2019 black Jaguar. A nice, pretty baby. It doesn't look like anyone is there but, I just sit for a moment and look, scheme and try to figure out a way to run up in this crib. I'll take my time with this. I think I'm a pay Chicago to watch his every move so the minute he sees Cee-Cee and Pete together he can call me. Yeah! That's what I'll do. We'll watch his every move and then it's a wrap.

I drive off to *Wicked*, give Chicago the money and tell him exactly what everything is hitting for. We agree on another hundred bands for the surveillance work and I bounce. It feels good to know that I'm finally gonna crack the case and that Cee-Cee is in for the shock of her life.

It's been two weeks, and this nigga hasn't even shown up at his crib. Did he go on a vacation or something? I don't know, but I'm getting frustrated. I speak to Cee-Cee every day, so I know he ain't with her. Where the fuck could this nigga be? I paid Chicago for another two weeks stake-out, so hopefully this nigga will show up.

It is damn near close to the fourth week and this muthafucka just showed up. Chicago calls me immediately and me and my brothers roll over there. When we pull up, I rush to Chicago's car, pay him and tell him, "We'll handle it from here."

My brothers and I, Kenny, Rick, Craig and Fred walk to the side door. Rick takes out his device to unlock the side door. After he gets it open, we enter and quietly close the door behind us. We walk through the kitchen, dining room, living room and sitting room. The place is quiet. We walk up a flight of stairs and while we are looking around, we suddenly hear movement and talking. We stand in front of the door to the room and listen attentively to the conversation. Wait a minute! It sounds like he's talking to Cee-Cee. In fact, he is talking to Cee-Cee. My blood is boiling now and I'm about to spaz. As he hangs up the phone, I bulldoze into the room, slap the fuck out of him with the back of my gun and knock him out immediately. Me and my brothers tape him up and ransack his whole house, looking for drugs, guns and money. We can't find anything, so we carry his body downstairs, drive the car up the driveway and put his ass in the trunk. We get back in the truck and drive to one of my spots down by the pier. When we get there, we carry Pete's dead weight ass into a secluded room that is soundproof. We strip his ass butt naked, bend him over a table, spread his arms and legs apart and cuff him to the table legs. I duct tape his mouth and wake his bitch-ass up.

"Pussy! Yo Pussy! Get the fuck up!"

I throw ice cold water in his face and slap him real hard…so hard that my fucking hand is on fire. Pete's head moves slowly from side to side and his eyes seem to be focusing. As soon as he realizes it's me, his eyes widen and he has a sudden look of fear on his face.

"Listen bitch. You know who I am. If you don't know, then I'm sure you heard about me. I know you are fucking my woman Cee-Cee. I also know you are helping Cee-Cee distribute her shit so, if you want me to spare your life today, when I take the tape off, you are going to tell me where she's at. Is that my child or yours? And who is Cee-Cee's main supplier? If you don't answer, then you will be tortured in the worst way. Okay?"

I take the tape off Pete's mouth and Pete swears to God that he don't know what I'm talking about. I slap flames out his ass and gun butt his jaw. Blood and teeth fly out of his mouth, and he cries in agony.

"Yo nigga!" Pete manages to say. "I don't know no Cee-Cee, no baby, and no supplier. Are you sure you got the right nigga? I just came back from a trip, so I'm kind of lost and this is not making any sense."

"Are you trying to play me? I just heard you talking to Cee-Cee in your house and now you wanna play dumb? Ok, have it your way. You wanna be loyal to this bitch? Well, let's see how loyal you are in a minute."

I signal for Fred to let Shantel and Merk to come in. I tell them, "Yall know what to do." Shantel gets in front of Pete, so he can see her. She then crawls under the table, sits on her ass and starts sucking on Pete's dick. Pete's hands are bawled up in a fist and he tries to restrain himself from getting a hard on, but he can't. Shantel is deep throating his dick. She yells out, "It's hard as a rock and tastes real good," and continues to suck his dick. I walk up to him and say, "You like that, don't you? Well, how does it feel to be sucked off by a man? I knew you were gay. I wonder if Cee-Cee knows that the nigga she's fucking is gay. Look at you! You look like you are ready to cum.

This is your last chance to speak so you better speak now or forever hold your peace."

"I tell you man! I don't know what you are talking about."

"Okay. Have it your way. Go ahead Merk. No mercy. I wanna hear screams."

Merk walks up behind Pete, pulls down his pants and jerk his eleven-inch dick to a full erection. He slaps it across Pete's ass cheeks and puts it between the crack of his ass. Pete's eyes pop out of his head and he screams, "No!" but it's too late. I'm not trying to hear shit from him now. The only thing I wanna hear are his screams. Merk commences to pushing all eleven inches of hard dick into Pete's ass. While Pete screams his head off, Merk continuously rams eleven inches of hard cock and Shantel has all of his dick in her mouth.

"Yo boss! This ass is extra tight. Do you want me to stop or can I live in it for a minute? I haven't had virgin ass since the pens, so will you let me work this?"

"Be my guest. He ain't tell me shit anyway, so tear it up. I wanna see him cry. I want him to speak in tongues and Shantel, don't stop sucking him off."

Merk is happy as a muthafucka. He digs all up in Pete's ass for an hour. He cums, walks around for a while and then goes back in. Pete screams, cries and not to mention, he bust five times in Shantel's mouth and every time his dick gets soft, Shantel sucks it back to a full erection. He can't help it, and I know his ass is starting to get loose. I thought about killing him immediately, but Merk is having too much fun. Besides, he's slowly dying with Merk's AIDS all up in his ass. I'm a let this torture go on for days.

I tell Merk, "I'm a leave him cuffed up here. Only give this nigga water. In the meantime, I'm a have other niggas come through and penetrate his ass." Since he says his ass is that good, then I might as well get paid off of it. "Finish doing what you're doing and then clean his asshole up. Have it nice and greased for the next man to dig into. If he decides to talk, call me immediately and if anyone takes the cuffs off this nigga, they will be shot dead."

I walk back over to Pete and say, "Are you ready to talk?"

"Kill me. Don't wait. kill me!" he shouts.

"Nah son. That would be too easy. You had the chance to spare your life, and you didn't so, now I'm a make sure you wish you were dead. Have fun!"

I walk out with my brother and we bounce. I thought about calling Cee-Cee but fuck her. Her time is coming slowing but surely. She just don't know.

The last five days have been really relaxing. I didn't call Cee-Cee, nor did I answer her calls. I just did me. I am driving over to the pier to find out what's up since I haven't gotten any calls. When I walk in the spot, it's smells funky as shit. Merk comes over and give me five grand and says, "Niggas been fucking Pete's ass all day and night. He is no good now."

"Is he still alive?"

"Yeah, he is. After the second day, there was no more screams. He just stared the other way and took all of the penetration. Big dicks and small dicks. Whatever came, he took. We also had to beat him up a bit. The nigga acted like he didn't want to suck no dick. But now, he opens his mouth with no problems. I guess he don't want no more ass whippings. He looks a mess also. His face is all dried up with semen."

I walk around to face him, and for sure, he is a mess. His eyes are closed and I assume he's asleep. I yell at him, "Yo nigga get up. Are you ready to talk now?" He slowly opens his eyes and says, "Kill me."

I get so mad and frustrated that I take out my razor and slice buck fifties all over his body. I get some rubbing alcohol, throw it all over him and then pour salt in his wounds. Pete screams until he passes out. I put some smelling salts under his nose to wake him up. When he does, he continues to scream, "Kill me! Kill me!"

I beat him and beat him, breaking all of his ribs. I uncuff him, tie him up, and put him in my trunk. Merk and I drive out to Jones Beach in Long Island and dump his naked ass on the sand, leaving him for dead. I drive off and head back to Queens…back to business. I didn't get to find out what I wanted to know, but I still have faith that I'll find Cee-Cee. One thing for sure, her middleman is dead.

Chapter Thirty-Four

Scared Shook

Damn! It's been two months since I heard from Pete. He called me as soon as he got back from the Bahamas, and that was it. Buddy has been calling me like crazy because he can't reach him either. Did he get arrested? Is he alive or what? I don't have Danny's information, so I don't know if he heard from him or not and Danny owes me, so what is really going on? This is freaking me out. I'm due next month and I don't need this stress. Man, I'm just going to take it easy until the dynamic trio get here. In three more weeks, we will all be reunited again. WOW! That's cool. I haven't seen Brother and C-note in a long time, due to my hot ass. I fucked everything up. It's all good now because everything is basically back to normal. Since I've been handling my business with Stan and Danny, I've managed to make a hundred million. I feel so good about that and so will they. All our money combined is damn near two hundred million, so our business plan is working. Billionaires is the title that we're claiming.

As weeks go by and still no word from Pete, I begin to get restless and nervous. The baby is kicking my ass and I need to get some air. My men will be here next week, so I need to do some shopping. I wanna have nice things prepared for them. Plus, I wanna get some sexy lingerie and sex the time away until the baby comes. I bet a hard dick inside of me would iron out all my pains. Yeah, that would do the job, as for right now, I'm a head over to Riverhead Outlet. I can get mad shit over there.

I jump in my Escalade and head out to Riverhead. The ride is as least an hour long, but I'm okay. As soon as I reach my destination, I park the truck and walk towards the Coach store. I glance in the window and I can't help myself, I must go in. I pick up a pair or burnt orange four-inch stilettos ankle boots with the matching tight-fitted jacket and bag to match. As I am cashing out my items, I spot an ill pair of glasses to go with them. Damn, this shit is hot. After leaving the Coach store, I walk down a couple of stores to Fendi. I go in and pick up some more shit. While coming out of Fendi and walking towards the Timberland store, who do I think I see? Tony! This nigga looks right in my direction. I turn my head fast and haul ass to the Nike store. I speed walk to the back of the store and hide there for a minute. I pray and pray that it's not him. Oh God! This cannot be happening to me. I'm so scared. How am I gonna make it to the truck? Is it him or not? He's not running after me, so it must have not been him. I know, for a fact, that if that was Tony, he would have run me down, dragged me to his car and terrorized my ass. I creep out from the back and look through the big windowpane. Everything appears to be normal. Maybe, I'm just being paranoid. Yeah! Scared, shook, scared to look. I think this is enough shopping for the day, but I'm too scared to leave the building.

I come out and look both ways but I don't see him. I walk back to the Timberland store and peek in. Damn, what's going on? All this excitement has my stomach growling and the baby is kicking the shit out of me. I walk up to the food mart and go to Micky D's. I order a bacon double-cheeseburger, super-size fries, vanilla shake and two apple pies. I sit down at the table and eat. While eating, my eyes are all over the place. This paranoid shit is making feel sick. I hurry up and eat my food, then haul ass out of there. I'm damn near running and looking back at the same time until I run into a group of women and I knock over their shit. As I stumble on top of their things, I apologize a hundred times. I look up at one of the women and say to her, "You look so familiar. Do I know you?"

She says, "No," and offers to help me to my truck.

We walk to my truck. I get in and thank her while slowly driving off. I cruise the whole parking lot looking to see if I can spot one of Tony's whips. I drive around and around, but I can't find any of his cars. I realize it was just me. I head out the exit and drive home.

When I get in front of my place, a feeling of relief comes over me. I am happy, but very exhausted. I decide to stay in for the next week and just wait for the men to arrive. The baby is ready to come and I need to take it easy. I don't want to deliver without C-note. He needs to be here. Besides, going out of the house makes me hallucinate.

Chapter Thirty-Five

Anxious

Today, I get to go home and make love to my wife. I can't wait to get there. All day yesterday, I spoke to her, and we talked about everything we are going to do. Cee-Cee said she has a very special gift for me and I'm dying to see it. I know she's as big as a house but I don't care. She is still sexy to me.

At eleven am, these people are letting me out. I don't know why I gotta wait so long, but hey, I'm not complaining. Better late than never. I got a limo waiting outside for me so I'll get home as quickly as possible. I'm really trying to get there before Brother and Buddy. If I could have at least twenty minutes with Cee-Cee, then my day won't seem so long. Damn, I'm nervous. I have never been so nervous. I can't believe the way I feel right now. In fact, what I'm feeling is more like a disturbing feeling. I hope everything is alright. My stomach is getting queasy and I feel like I can't breathe. I think I'm going to lay down.

After laying down for about an hour and a half, I wake up just in time to hear my name being called. I have to report to R&D. Yeah, it's time to bounce. I give my niggas pounds n' shit and haul ass to

R&D. After going through the formalities, I am released and jet to the limo.

Yes, I'm finally on my way to Yepton Mansion. I should be there by two. It all depends on traffic. I'm a lean back and let the driver do his thing. I feel real intense and it's scaring me. I'll have the driver wake me up when we're almost there.

Chapter Thirty-Six

Brother & Buddy

Well finally, I'm about to shine. It's been a long time since I've seen my family or my house and I can't wait to slide up in some hot pussy. I know my sister is having a baby and all, but she'll understand that a nigga got to do what a nigga got to do. I wonder what hoe I'm a break down tonight. Yeah! Shit is not a game. Me and Buddy can hang out tonight. We'll find some girls. I got a whole list of them lined up, so it's on. I hope Cee-Cee doesn't have no long, dragged-out dinner tonight. As soon as I get there, we'll chill for an hour, then go shopping and then I'll see sis when the baby comes. Seven-day furlough. You know I'm a be off the chain. Buddy, too. Cee-Cee shouldn't even care anyway because her and C-note will be in their own little world. I'll be lucky if they even notice me.

Hold up! Do I hear my muthafucking name being paged to R&D? Yeah, that's what I'm talking about. Get me the fuck up on out of here.

I walk my ass to R&D, do the necessary paperwork and step outside. First thing I see is Buddy looking sharp as a muthafucka, driving a champagne Bugatti. I hop in that bad boy and say, "It's time to party."

Yes indeed, we are on our way to Yepton mansion.

Chapter Thirty-Seven

Cee-cee's Visitors

Today, is the happiest day of my life. Brother, C-note and Buddy will all be here. Buddy flew out to PA last night and slept out there to pick up Brother this morning. C-note is being release at eleven so, everyone will be here around two. I hope C-note gets here before they do, so we can get buck wild a little bit. Damn, I need that, and I know he needs it too. Yesterday, he called me all day, every hour on the hour and I was turned the fuck on. I promise myself I wouldn't masturbate because I want him to have all of me. I love my man. I am so glad that Tony and I aren't conversing anymore. The way that we eased up off each other was the ideal thing to do. This way, there's no animosity or conflict. I know this is his baby, but I'm sure he'll get over it and move on. It don't make sense to hang on to something that's not there. Even though I love him, I'm not *in love* with him. To be honest, he was only good to satisfy my needs. Yes, he did please the pussy but so does C-note and I'm in love with him. I will never fuck on C-note again. It just caused too many problems and niggas don't know how to act. It's crazy. Point blank, I'm just glad he is not in my life anymore.

Ding-dong! My doorbell rings. Who could that be? No one ever rings my doorbell. I look out my window and I see a box truck that's reads "Flowers for you" on the side. Aww, did C-note have roses sent to me? This is so nice. I walk down the stairs with Pus-Pus in my arms and open the door. When I open the door, I'm greeted with the hardest slap ever that knocked Pus-Pus out of my hands as I land on the floor. I look up in amazement and it's the bitch from the parking lot at Riverhead. What the fuck is she doing and why is she here? As I try to crawl to get up, this bitch grabs me by my hair and pulls me up. She drags me up the stairs to my bedroom and throws me inside. I turn around to ask what is going on and four other females appears at her side. These bitches are tall, exotic and dangerous-looking. I know they are not here to talk or play games.

The woman who slapped me says, "Listen bitch! I don't want to kill you. You're pregnant n' shit, so let's make this real easy. Okay! First off, I know who you are, so please don't act like you are this innocent bitch. As you already know by the looks of us, we are the Bronx Stick Up Chicks. All we want is the money, drugs, and jewelry. Just give us everything and we will not hurt you."

"It's just me and my cat that live here. My people are on their way and they can better assist you. All I have is a thousand dollars. There are no drugs, money and no jewelry here but what you see on me. I'm due to have my baby any day now so please don't hurt me. I'm telling you the truth."

Hysterically I begin to cry holding my belly, but they were not hearing that shit. The girl who slapped me must be the leader of this crew because she is the only one talking. She walks up to me and slap me repeatedly and told the other girls to lay me down on the bed, spread eagle and tie my arms and legs to the bed post. My body is exposed because I slept naked last night and I had just put a robe on when I heard the doorbell.

The leader stands over me and slaps me some more and yells and screams at me to give up the goods. I yell and scream back, "I don't know what you're talking about." With all the crying and stress, I begin to get sharp pains in my stomach. The other girls left my room to search my house. I can hear then moving shit, throwing shit on the floor, breaking up shit and them cursing up a storm. The leader comes back into the room and stands in front of me again and the more I look at her, the more I think I know her, but I just can't place her face. She leans over to me and whispers, "You think you know I am?"

I look at her in shock because it's like this bitch is reading my mind.

"No," I say.

She sticks her tongue in my mouth, then looks at me, now I am totally lost and confused. I move my head to get her tongue out of my mouth, but she holds my face, squeezes my jaw and tongues me. Oh my God! I'm about to get raped by some broads. This is not happening to me today. I scream and cry for her to stop, but she just keeps on kissing me. She moves her tongue out of my mouth and starts sucking on my breasts. She sucks them so hard and pinches them that I cry out in pain. It's bad enough that they are sensitive. I hate it and it hurts. By the time she finishes sucking on them, they are so pointy they just stick straight up pointing to the ceiling.

"Please stop," I beg, but she keeps right on, and her head goes lower and lower until I can't see her anymore. My belly is blocking my view, but I can feel a wet tongue on my clit and she is moving her tongue so fast on my clit my body begins to shake. I do not want to respond to her mess, but I can't front, it feels so good. She teases my clit some more before she sticks her tongue inside and tongue-fucks me for a while. She goes back to my clit and gives me incredible head. I think she knows I am enjoying it, and before I know it, I cum. I cum so hard that I shake uncontrollably. When she finishes sucking up all my juices, she looks at me and I notice all her lipstick is gone. *I know this girl*, I keep saying to myself. Think! Think! Think! But her face won't come into play. Her friends are back and say, "We found something in the linen closet." She leaves, but she comes right back and says, "What's the security code to the vault?"

"What vault?"

"I'm a ask you one last time. What's the security code for the vault?"

"Lady, I don't know what you're talking about."

The leader jumps on top of me and starts slapping me over and over until my face feels like it on fire and I'm bleeding from my mouth and nose. She tells the other girls to look in every closet to find more numeric keypads. They leave out again and this girl is just punishing my face. All I can do is lay here. I can't move, can't see and can't talk, but I can hear them saying that they found another keypad in my closet. They're fumbling with it trying every number, name and everything they can think of, but no success. They won't ask me anymore questions because I am damn near dead. I squint to look at the time and its noon. I pray to God that he keeps me alive for the next two hours but I don't know if I can make it. I'm beaten up bad. I don't care what happens to me, but I just want my baby to survive.

It's twelve-thirty and these bitches are going ballistic. My eyes are closed but I can hear them. I feel little rough licks on my face and ticklish pricks by my nose. I open my eyes a little and see that it is Pus-Pus. I am so happy to see my cat that I begin to cry. If I had any strength left in my body, I would tell her to go away.

The leader comes back over to me and unties my hands and ankles. I lay here in so much pain, I can't move. Pus-Pus stays by my side and keeps licking my face. The vision in one of my eyes clears up. I look around and see that my room is a total mess. They are in my closet breaking up shit. The leader steps back out and looks around my room. She stares at me for a minute and then she looks at Pus-Pus. Her eyes are going back and forth, from me to Pus-Pus. She walks over and grabs her. She lifts her up in the air and notice a diamond collar with a platinum heart charm around her neck. On one side of the heart are eighteen numbers in diamonds and on the other side is the name BUDDY. The leader takes the collar off Pus-Pus's neck and stares at it. While her friends are still tearing shit up, she sits with Pus-Pus and looks at the charm. She stares at the charm for about ten minutes until something finally clicks in her head. She gets up, walks over to the closet and shouts to the girls to punch in the name BUDDY. The girls do, but it declines the name. They keep trying the name again and again, but it keeps rejecting it. The leader now reads out the numbers on the front of the charm and when the last number is hollered out, the wall moves. All I can hear is a bunch of screaming and cheering. Their voices even sound different. They run out of the room, and five minutes later I hear another set of cheers. They must have opened the second vault.

It's now one o'clock and time is moving very slow. My face hurts and my breathing is shallow. I'm fucked up and I can't move. Suddenly, a gush of water flows between my legs with excruciating pains. I lazily look around and I can see are the girls moving my money out of my room. This is bad, very bad and I'm slowly dying. "God please help me," I pray.

While lying there praying, the leader comes up to me and says, "It's time for me to go now. Thank you. Thank you for making me so fucking rich. I should kill you, but by the looks of it, you're dying anyway."

She puts my arms around her neck and kisses me again. As my hands fall from her neck and back to my side, I manage to pull her wig off. "Oh my God! It's you," and the leader gives me the hardest blow to my head.

Chapter Thirty-Eight

Disaster

Well, it's about time. I'm finally here. In the next four minutes, I'll be pulling up in my driveway. Everything in the area looks the same. It's quiet and homely. I hope Cee-Cee is waiting outside for me. Damn, every time I mention her name, I get nervous. I hope she didn't deliver already. I wanna be there, helping her push. As we get closer to my driveway, a box truck almost crashes into the limo, jetting off at top speed. Aww, that must be the surprise she was talking about. I probably got rose pedals leading up to the bedroom. Yeah, Cee-Cee would do something like that. I am yearning to dig up in that ass. As we turn in. I hear a horn blowing behind me like crazy. I look back and see it's Brother and Buddy. Damn! No ass 'til tonight but the family reunion can get started now. We pull up to the entrance and get out. We hug, give each other pounds and shout for Cee-Cee. We're kind of surprised that she isn't outside especially with all the noise we are making. Brother walks over to the door and punches in the security number.

The door opens up and we all freeze in shock when we see Pus-Pus hanging from the ceiling with her neck broke. We slowly walk in like, "What the fuck?" Everything is a mess. All the furniture is smashed and destroyed. I call out for Cee-Cee, but she still does not answer. I run up the stairs like a lunatic, kick open my bedroom door and see my wife lying there bloody, sprawled out and not moving. I yell frantically for Brother and Buddy and they come rushing in. Buddy immediately picks up the phone and dials 911. This is the Hamptons so the ambulance will be here within five minutes. We kneel over her, crying like children trying to wake her up, but she won't.

When the paramedics pulls up and run up the stairs, they go straight to Cee-Cee, check her pulse and say…

Stay Tuned!!!

Ownership with a Vengeance

ABOUT THE AUTHOR

Camo was born in Manhattan New York. Currently she resides in Groveland, Florida with her husband and four sons. While working as a Certified Medical Coder, she manages to pursue her number one passion, creative writing. After releasing her first title, "Ownership," she is currently filled with pleasure and excitement in anticipation of the release of the sequel.

CPSIA information can be obtained
at www.ICGtesting.com
Printed in the USA
LVHW110240121119
636959LV00002BA/640/P